Penny Dolan is a children's writer and storyteller. *The Third Elephant* was inspired by a miniature Taj Mahal brought all the way back from India long, long ago by her grandmother – and the magnificence of elephants, of course. Her other books include *The Tale of Rickety Hall* (nominated for the Children's Book Award), *The Ghost of Able Mabel* (World Book Day 2004 Recommended Read) and various picture book stories, including *Mr Pod and Mr Piccalilli* with Nick Sharratt. Penny is a popular Book Week visitor in schools and libraries and at other literacy events. She lives in North Yorkshire, and has three untidy desks, two grown-up children and one rather bad cat.

Books by the same author

The Tale of Rickety Hall
The Tale of Highover Hill
The Tale of White Winter Hollow
The Ghost of Able Mabel
The Spectre of Hairy Hector
The Phantom of Billy Bantam
The Ghoul of Bodger O'Toole

The Third Elephant

PENNY DOLAN

Illustrated by Helen Craig

**WALKER
BOOKS**

This is a work of fiction. Names, characters, places and incidents are
either the product of the author's imagination or, if real, are used fictitiously.

First published 2007 by Walker Books Ltd
87 Vauxhall Walk, London SE11 5HJ

2 4 6 8 10 9 7 5 3 1

Text © 2007 Penny Dolan
Illustrations © 2007 Helen Craig

The right of Penny Dolan and Helen Craig to be identified as author and illustrator
respectively of this work has been asserted by them in accordance with the Copyright,
Designs and Patents Act 1988

This book has been typeset in Perpetua

Printed and bound in Great Britain by Creative Print and Design (Wales), Ebbw Vale

British Library Cataloguing in Publication Data:
a catalogue record for this book
is available from the British Library

ISBN 978-1-4063-0082-6

www.walkerbooks.co.uk

For Louisa Annie Rose & Evelyn Gladys Richardson —
To their Great-Great-Grandchildren,
all my love. P.D.

IN THE BEGINNING

IN THE BEGINNING

LARGE TREES HID THE OLD HOUSE from the street lights. Boards barricaded up the empty basement, and scaffolding reached to the roof gutters. Only one large window, high on the third floor, still faced the sky.

Moonlight peered in through the grimy window-panes. It moved across the faded wallpaper, over the shabby furniture and the silent piano, until it reached a narrow shelf, a little below the ceiling.

On that shelf stood three carved wooden elephants. They seemed to be setting out on a long journey, but dust lay across their backs like worn velvet. How long had they been there? They could not remember.

The first was definitely the largest and the second was certainly middle-sized, but the third elephant was exactly the right size to stand on the palm of an out-stretched hand.

As the moonlight lit the shelf, something seemed to glint in the eyes of the smallest elephant. Slowly, behind the wooden trunk, his carved mouth seemed to curve in a small, cheering smile. Below him, down on the lid of the piano, stood a miniature marble palace, whiter than the moonlight that flickered around it. Elegant minarets graced each corner, and the beautiful dome was tipped with gold. It was a palace fit for dreams.

"Will you ... will you tell me about the beautiful palace?" asked the third elephant.

"Sssh! Sssh!" replied a pair of quick, cross voices. "Small elephants should be seen and not heard."

"Please?" he begged.

"One day, one day," they said, as they always did.

The small elephant sighed, but he went on looking at the palace, because it made him happy to see it. He dreamed on, and time passed, and the moonlight moved across the floor.

A grey mouse darted out from a crack in the skirting board. It ran across the floorboards and dashed up the piano leg. It sat on the once-polished lid, with its grey head on one side, looking at the palace too.

The mouse twitched its tail and glanced up. "Still here, small elephant?"

The third elephant smiled down at the mouse. "Where else could I go?"

All he had ever known was this room and the changing sky beyond. He knew there must be other places, but the two big elephants never spoke of such things.

The grey mouse twirled around, chasing the loops of its tail. Then it looked up again. "Do you never wish for more, little one?" it asked.

"More?" said the elephant. "What sort of more?"

The mouse shrugged. "Whatever more you want to wish for, I suppose. What do you want? What do you dream about?"

Before the small elephant could answer, the house creaked loudly. A thin crack scratched its way across the ceiling and along a wall. The mouse skittered down to the floor, its whiskers twitching. "I suggest you wish very soon indeed," it said, trembling slightly.

The small elephant's smile seemed to fade into shadow. "Will you be in my wish, mouse?" he asked.

"Who knows? Just be brave and wish, little one," the mouse called, scampering away. It left a trail of footprints in the dust.

So the small elephant returned his gaze to the palace, still floating in its pool of moonlight. "If I had a wish," he thought, "the lovely white palace would certainly be in it." But why had the mouse told him to wish soon? "Excuse me…" he began.

"Hush!" rumbled the largest wooden elephant. "Not now."

"Peace and quiet is what we need!" added the second elephant.

It was no use asking them, ever. Sometimes the room was so full of peace and quiet that it hurt.

Later that morning, a large van spluttered into the overgrown drive. Men clambered out of the van, panting in the late summer heat. They trudged up the stairs. They took away the furniture. They took away the white palace. They took away the piano too, which was difficult to carry. By the time the piano was safely in the van, the men had forgotten about the three elephants.

The big elephants did not like the men disturbing them.

"Please, what is happening?" the small elephant asked.

"Hush, hush, HUSH!" they scolded angrily. "We've had enough noise for one day!"

When night came, the small elephant looked at the empty pool of moonlight. He thought about what the mouse had told him: wish for what you want, wish for what you dream about.

"I wish," he thought, as hard as he could, "I wish I could see the white palace again."

The moonlight flickered around the room like secret laughter.

Next day, an awful noise began. It grew louder and louder, as if someone or something were striking against the old house. Spiders dropped from the cornice, and ran off between the floorboards. The walls shivered, the floors shook. Grating, grinding noises came up from the street. The hot summer air was full of dust.

The two large elephants grumbled and groaned. "We must have peace and quiet," they muttered.

Another man came crashing up the stairs. He barged into the forgotten room, carrying a crowbar. A smell of sweat and beer came with him. He had come to see if there was still anything worth taking. As he turned to leave, he spotted the high shelf, and the three carved figures.

"What are you doing up there?" he mocked, and knocked the first elephant down from the shelf, and then the second. A siren shrieked a warning.

"Too late, poor jumbos!" the man roared, laughing.

"You're probably full of woodworm anyway." He tossed the big elephant, and then the middle-sized elephant through a smashed window.

"Oy! Watch out for flying elephants!" he shouted, joking with his mates below.

The two elephants fell through billowing brick-dust, down to the rubble heaps surrounding the broken house.

As the siren screamed again, the demolition man knocked the third elephant down too. He hurled the small carving through the window. "Here's a little one for luck!" he roared.

Now, maybe he was just that much smaller, or maybe the man threw harder, or maybe something magical happened, but suddenly the small elephant found himself flying through the air in a great arc.

He soared over the demolition gang, over the machines and trucks below, and into the huge trees. He tumbled between branch and branch, past shimmering summer leaves and twittering birds. Then he fell down, down, down.

SARA

A s SARA RACED DOWN THE STREET, desperately late, something whooshed through the leaves above her head. Without thinking, she reached out and caught something. But what?

She opened her hands, and saw a small, carved elephant smiling at her. She stared up at the thick canopy of branches, wondering where the creature had come from.

A woman barged past, talking loudly on her mobile, and Sara remembered she was in a hurry herself.

"Who you are and how you got here, I don't know, small elephant," she said, "but now you're coming with me to see the scariest music teacher in the world."

Sara stood in the dreaded room. She was hot from running the last two blocks.

Most music teachers took the summer off, but not Mr Green. He had had his three weeks away, and now he was back. He insisted that he had time to give Sara some extra lessons, and Mum agreed at once, because he was the best teacher around.

"You're lucky that he asked you!" Mum had said.

Sara didn't feel lucky. She loved her flute, but she certainly didn't love Mr Green. He was terrifying. And, right now, Mr Green's bushy white eyebrows met in a frown.

"Show me!" he said sharply. Sara held out the small, carved figure. "No, not that. Put it down, and show me your fingers, you silly girl! Are they all right?"

Sara put the wooden elephant on the mantelpiece, among stacks of CDs and old concert tickets. Then she held out her hands. Mr Green turned them this way and that.

"They seem fine," his wife said, peering over his shoulder and smiling at Sara. "Don't make such a fuss."

"Fine? Fine? Hmmph!" he growled. "What if she'd damaged her fingers catching that thing? I'd have no pupil. She'd have no chance of playing at the Celebration Concert. My work would be wasted, and all because of a lump of old wood." He scowled over his glasses. "If you want me to give you lessons, Miss Saraswati, you must take care of your hands. Do you understand?"

Sara nodded uncertainly. She absolutely hated being told off.

"Now, please play."

Sara lifted her flute, but her heart was beating too fast. Mr Green was always angry when she was late. He'd got even angrier when she explained about the elephant, and now ... now, she couldn't even concentrate.

"Sorry," she whispered, a blush spreading across her pale brown cheeks.

"Start again," Mr. Green ordered, gruffly.

It was no good. Her breathing was too tight to play a note. Maybe he'd cancel her lessons, throw her out, declare her useless, after all? And he was the best teacher around, wasn't he? Sara looked desperately, blankly, across to the mantelpiece, and then her eyes rested on the small elephant.

The small wooden elephant saw Sara too. He saw her silvery flute, and her curtain of dark hair. After the awful silence of the old house, he longed to hear something lovely.

"Go on, Sara," he thought. "Let me listen. Play, please play!"

And at that moment, Sara noticed the odd little smile on the elephant's carved face, and felt more cheerful too.

Play? she thought. *Yes, I can play, and I will play. Not for you, old Grumbly Mr Green, but for my funny wooden elephant.* She beamed back at the animal, and this time put the flute steadily to her lips.

As Sara's calm, clear notes echoed round the studio, Mr Green relaxed. He nodded gently to himself, watching the concentration on her face.

Yes. Maybe this girl *was* as good as he had hoped. She had worked hard last term and was playing well now, even after his holiday. Perhaps he *would* put her name forward for the Celebration Concert — as long as she used her brains in future, and didn't make a habit of catching hard wooden objects, no matter how charming they were. He eyed the miniature elephant grimly.

Sara raced upstairs to the flat. Mum wasn't home from work yet, but a soft voice called out, "How did your lesson go?"

"Brilliant!" Sara called back. "Look what I've got, Nanji."

The third elephant found himself handed to a golden old lady, seated on a large sofa. Her hair was greying a little, but her dark eyes danced, just like her granddaughter's. As Sara described how he had fallen from the trees by the old house, Nanji turned the animal round admiringly.

"He is beautifully carved," she said, "but he needs a good clean, don't you think? Fetch me that special oil from the cupboard over there — and a soft cloth."

Soon the small elephant was smooth and glossy. Nanji's oil had taken away the layers of stale, damp dust. Every carefully carved wrinkle in his skin gleamed.

"Can I put him in your golden corner for now?"

Sara asked. "I want Mum to see him."

"Certainly. A lucky place for a lucky elephant."
Nanji smiled. "Then you can make me a nice pot of
tea, and tell me about your music lesson."

Carefully, Sara put the small elephant on her grandmother's table, next to the brass tray where Nanji
kept her prayer candles and incense box.

The elephant stared at the cloth of golden silk
spread beneath his feet, and the scented freesias in the
vase beside him. From here, he watched Sara in the
kitchen, filling the kettle. He saw Nanji, among her
comfortable cushions, marking the last papers in a
pile. He saw the green leaves of potted palms, and the
shelves full of books. He could not remember being in
a room where people actually lived before.

Then the small elephant glanced upwards, and was
even more amazed. On the wall above the golden
table was a painting of a wonderful blue man with a
flute in his hands. He was dancing in a magical forest,
and all kinds of animals were gathered around, listening to his music. The small elephant gazed at the man's
playful face, and a strange feeling came over him. He
felt sad that there was no elephant in the blue flute-
player's marvellous forest.

"Hello! I'm home," called a voice from the hallway.

"Mum!" Sara grinned, putting another mug on the
tray.

Her mother struggled in, and dumped down a
bulging briefcase. She slipped off her coat, shook out

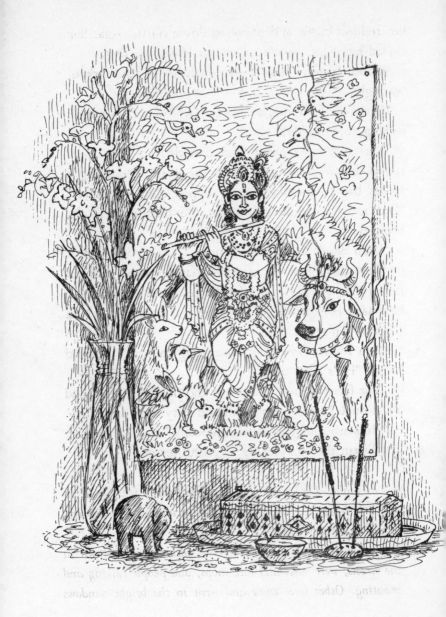

her reddish curls, and plumped down on the sofa. She closed her eyes, and leant against Nanji, smiling.

"Good day, my dear daughter-in-law?" Nanji asked, teasingly.

"Good to be home, mama-in-law!" Mum answered, sighing contentedly.

"Me too!" A teenage girl bounded in, her spiky cropped hair still damp from the gym. She flung a sports bag to the floor, and slipped off her trainers. "Did my best time so far on the bike today!" she crowed.

"Well done, Nita, " said Mum.

The small elephant saw that Sara did not rush to find a mug for her big sister. Instead, she let her dark hair hang over her face, as if she was waiting for Nita to greet her, too.

"Sara found something interesting today," remarked Nanji. "He's over there."

Four faces turned to stare at the third elephant, and all at once he felt very small and very shy.

"He's my lucky wooden elephant," Sara explained, and began the story of the dreadful lesson.

It was night. The small elephant stood on a windowsill in Sara's bedroom. As she breathed gently under her bedcovers, he gazed happily out.

He saw planes tracing across the darkened sky. Down in the streets, were cars, and late shops, and people talking and shouting. Other lives came and went in the bright windows

opposite. So much to see, he thought. Then the night clouds parted, and the moon was there too, glowing, just as before.

There was a quick scrabbling, and a tiny, whiskered face appeared on the sill. Eyes twinkling, a grey mouse scurried towards him. "How are you, then?" he said. "Do you like your new home?"

"Are you my mouse?" asked the elephant. "The mouse from the house?"

The visitor shook his furry head. "No, I'm not. I'm his hundredth nephew. Word travels fast in the mouse world."

"Yes! Now I can see that your tail is much longer," the elephant said, politely.

The mouse gave his tail an elegant twirl, "Uncle asked us to keep an eye out for you on our scrabbles. And I'm the one who found you! Hooray! More cheese back at the nest for me!" he squeaked. "Oh, by the way, I forgot to ask. Are you happy? Uncle wanted to know."

"Yes," the elephant said, smiling.

"Good. Uncle said that you must remember – oh dear! Remember what?" The mouse scratched a pink ear, then grinned. "Remember that this is only the beginning!"

"The beginning of what?" asked the small elephant.

"He didn't say. A dream? A wish? A journey?" The mouse gave a puzzled shrug, and was gone.

* * *

When morning came, the third elephant discovered there was not always peace and quiet in his new home. Sara was practising her scales.

"Stop that!" Nita yelled, bursting into the lounge with a phone pressed to her ear.

Sulkily, Sara lowered her flute. "What?"

"I'm trying to check my travel plans, and I can't hear a word with all your noise!" Nita cried.

"It's not noise! I have to do my scales, don't I?" Sara snapped back.

They faced each other, fury blazing in their eyes. Such different sisters, thought the small elephant – Sara, quiet and precise, dreaming of music and concerts, and long-legged Nita, buzzing with energy and dreaming of travelling in a faraway land.

Suddenly, the rage left Nita's eyes. She put down the phone and ran a hand through her spiky hair. She hugged her little sister tight. "Sorry. Didn't mean to lose it," Nita muttered. "Guess it's my cycling nerves again."

She glanced across at the family calendar on the wall. There, scribbled between Sara's music lessons and Mum's meetings, was a pair of circled dates. Nita's birthday and the day of the bike ride departure. One date after another, and only a month away!

"It's really soon, Nita," Sara said.

"Don't I know it?" Nita groaned. "The organizers were worried. I guess I'll be the youngest rider ever – my birthday's just before we go. Maybe I'll mess up, eh?"

Nita's eyes told Sara this wasn't her usual joking.

"You're mad!" Sara was astonished. How could her big sister be worried by this bike trip? "You're the best cyclist I know. You'll be fantastic. Better than any of them," she declared fiercely.

"Thanks." Nita laughed, giving Sara another hug. "Sorry for moaning at you. Friends again?"

"Yes."

"Get on with your scales then, kid. No excuses. I'll make my calls later," Nita said. "And keep practising while I'm away. I want to come home and hear you in that big concert, OK? Get your lucky elephant on the case."

Lucky elephant? Sara wasn't sure the wooden carving was really, truly lucky, but there must have been some magic around, because next day she got a letter from Mr Green.

"He hasn't just entered me to play at the Celebration Concert. He's put my name down for the final solo, too!" Sara shrieked, delighted.

"Hello," the mouse nephew said, nibbling on a lost peanut. "How are you getting on, small one?"

"She calls me her lucky elephant," the small elephant replied. "But what if I'm not? What if I'm ordinary?"

"Maybe if you think something's lucky, then it is?" suggested the mouse.

"Like that peanut?" asked the elephant, his eyes shining with fun. *"Think how lucky you were to find it!"*

"Pfffft!" the mouse spluttered, choking on the nut. He had to dart off before he woke Sara.

There were only two flute players down for the big solo. Miss Mackenzie, the concert organizer, introduced the two girls at a music workshop.

"Right, Sara and Lauren, I hope you'll help one another." Miss Mackenzie smiled. "You'll both need to study the solo. The panel will choose one of you to be the main soloist, and the other the reserve, just in case there are problems on the night. Do you understand?"

Sara understood that, but when Lauren sneered at her, and then tried to stare her into playing badly, she felt confused. If it hadn't been for the weight of the small wooden elephant, smiling away in her pocket, she'd have given up there and then. Somehow, thinking of his cheery grin, she got through the piece without any mistakes.

"That was excellent, Sara. Can you sound a little more joyful next time?" Miss Mackenzie beamed. "Thank you. Your turn now, Lauren."

Lauren didn't do so well. She shoved hard against Sara as they left the rehearsal hall.

As soon as Sara got home and into her bedroom, she leant forward, her chin in her hands, and faced the small, wooden carving.

"Did you really know I'd be chosen for the solo, little elephant? Did you?"

The elephant's eyes seemed to shine as he looked back at her. *I was wishing for you. That's all I do,* he seemed to say.

"But it worked, didn't it?" said Sara. "Maybe that's what Nanji would call elephant magic."

The days rushed by, and soon there was only one week before the bike ride. Nita was forever out training, or sitting at the computer on the landing, furiously checking her emails. Clothes and maps and cycling gadgets were scattered everywhere. There was hardly any space for anyone else. Sometimes Nita was full of jokes and friendliness, and sometimes her face was as menacing as a thundercloud.

One evening, while Sara squashed up next to her grandmother on the sofa, she asked. "Nanji, why's Nita so moody about this cycle thing? It's only a really long bike ride, isn't it?"

Nanji paused. "Ah, Sara. It's more than that. You were too young to know your daddy, but after my Sanjit's accident, poor little Nita missed him very, very much. We both know Nita is doing this sponsored bike ride for a very good cause. But I also think that, deep down, Nita wants to prove to her daddy that she can do it, even now he has gone. That's why doing it perfectly matters so much to her, my pet."

"So we must be kind to her even when she's moody," Sara stated, sighing deeply.

"Exactly," said Nanji. "Tough, isn't it?" And they both giggled.

After a while, Sara took the small elephant out to the hall, to where Mum kept the last family photo. It was on the wall by the front door, so it welcomed them all whenever they came home. Sara was thinking about what Nanji had told her.

"Look, small elephant," she told him. "There we all were."

The photo showed Dad, beaming proudly. He had one arm tightly hugged around Mum. In his other, he held a tiny baby Sara, wrapped in a new shawl. Clinging to Dad's side, as if she wanted to climb into his arms as well, was seven-year-old Nita. Beside them stood Nanji, smiling as calmly as ever.

Sara swallowed hard. "That was our daddy," she said softly. "Once upon a time."

At last, it was Nita's birthday, and the day before her flight. All morning, from the golden corner, the small elephant had watched Nanji bustling about in the kitchen. By late afternoon, delicious smells filled the flat. Now all was ready. As soon as they heard the front door slam, Sara and Mum carried dishes of spicy food to the long table.

"What's going on?" cried Nita, as she bounded up the stairs. "Something smells great!"

"It's for you!" shouted Sara.

"To wish you a happy birthday, and a good trip tomorrow, darling," said Mum, beaming.

"It was my idea, girl, so you had better enjoy your meal," said Nanji, wagging her finger sternly. "There'll be time to finish your packing afterwards."

Nita dashed off to wash. She came back wearing her best new top, and her biggest hoop earrings. She had tied a scarlet braid twice round her spiky hair, leaving the long ends dangling down her back.

"Nita looks really pretty," Sara thought, smiling. She'd woven the braid for her big sister last summer. It had taken ages.

Nita grinned at the colourful spread of dishes. "Thanks! You've made my favourites."

"Peace a moment, dear granddaughter," Nanji said, putting a finger on Nita's lips. "Good. Now I know you are modern and strong, but your journey will be all the better for a blessing." She led Nita towards the golden corner.

The small elephant watched as Nanji lit the little diva lamps on the brass tray beside him. She lit the incense sticks, too. Then, bowing her head, half chanting, half praying, she lifted the tray towards the picture of the blue man, and circled it gently. Threads of perfumed smoke spiralled into the air.

As she set down the tray, the divas flickered like petals of fire. Nanji seemed to gather the bright light within her two hands, lifting it in blessing to Nita's forehead. Then, with a final prayer, she took a blossom from the vase, and tucked it gently behind Nita's ear. "May the Lord protect you, my dear girl," she murmured.

Then she patted Nita's hand, and smiled. "And now it's time for your birthday feast!" They joined Mum and Sara, and began to eat.

Incense wafted around the small elephant; cumin and coriander filled the air, and bubbles of laughter burst from his new family as they chatted together. He looked up at the picture of the beautiful blue flute-player. *How little I know of the world*, he thought, and all at once the image of the lost white palace shimmered in his mind.

When the birthday meal was over, Sara took the small elephant up to her bedroom. Soon she heard Nita singing away in her own room, doing her last-minute packing.

The clock seemed to be ticking very fast.

*   *   *

 As soon as everything was quiet, the small mouse squeezed up onto the window sill. His cheeks were full of sugared fennel seeds, collected up after the feast. The elephant smiled, for today had been a happy day.

"I have a trick to show you, small elephant. I learnt it from my uncle." The mouse bent over and scattered the seeds as if they were tea-leaves, and he was telling a fortune. His whiskers quivered. "Aha! I see a journey coming," he whispered. "I see a long, long journey. I hope you are ready, my friend." Then he swept up the seeds and started nibbling them rapidly.

"Ready for what?" asked the small elephant, startled.

"The journey."

"That's not me," the elephant explained. "That's Nita."

"Is that so? Ah well, it never does anyone harm to wish them safe travelling," the mouse replied, darting towards a gap in the window frame. He paused, and waved a paw in a kindly way. "Goodbye, small elephant!"

In the middle of the night, Sara woke. Light was still shining under Nita's door. Sara softly pushed it open, and went in. She trod carefully around her sister's luggage.

"Are you all right?" she whispered.

"Yes. Go away!" mumbled the figure curled under the covers. "You're too young to understand."

"Nita, what is it? Tell me!" Sara said.

Nita's exhausted face peered out from the bundle of bedclothes. She lifted a hopeless hand towards the pin-board on the wall. The surface was covered with maps and charts and lists. In between were newspaper clippings showing Nita standing beside proud sponsors.

"What if I don't make it?" she said. "How will I face coming back? Meeting those people again?"

"You'll do it. I know you will. D for definitely!" Sara said, snuggling onto the bed beside her big sister. "And they'll all be really, really jealous because you'll be as fit as anything, and look all tanned and beautiful. Except," she added, laughing, "for a very sore bum and lots of insect bites."

Nita started laughing as well. "OK, Sara," she said. "Enough. I must go to sleep." Yawning, she closed her eyes. "I hope you're right," she muttered softly.

As Nita fell asleep, Sara lay thinking. At last, she slipped silently back to her own room.

She opened a drawer, found some sticky labels, and snipped a corner off one of them. She chose a water-proof pen, and in her very, very tidiest and tiniest letters, she wrote:

LUCKY ELEPHANT.
PLEASE RETURN.

Unpeeling the label, Sara turned the wooden elephant upside down – rather rudely, he thought – and stuck the scrap of paper firmly on. It was just the right size to fit under one back foot.

"You've been lucky for me," Sara said. "Be lucky for Nita, too." Tiptoeing back into her big sister's room, she thrust the carving into Nita's luggage. "Bye!" she whispered. "Bye, small elephant."

As Sara cuddled up in her own bed once more, she tried not to worry. She tried to block out any thoughts of the Celebration Concert. She would not think about it. She would not think about playing that solo without her lucky elephant. She would *not*. The concert was weeks away, not now, and it was now that Nita needed her luck.

The small elephant could hardly believe what was happening to him. He was jostled about in Nita's bag, squashed up against uncomfortable unknown objects, stuck next to unmentionable underwear, packs of plasters and odd-smelling tubes of foot balm. He heard goodbyes and shouts and strange, distorted voices.

Eventually, all the sounds became one deep, echoing roar. The elephant felt as if he were trapped in some place of terrible tightness, surging through currents of cold and heat for a long, long time.

"The mouse was right," he thought, a little afraid. "The journey has come after all."

NITA

As the third elephant tumbled out of Nita's luggage onto the bed, sunshine burst brightly around him, vibrant with the scent of spices and petrol fumes. They had arrived at a hostel in the middle of a busy city. He felt deafened by the rumble of vehicles and the shouts and calls of a dozen languages outside.

All the same, the small elephant smiled up at Nita, for that was what he was here for.

Nita's anxious eyes suddenly shone. "What on earth...?" she gasped, picking him up. She saw the scrap of paper stuck to his foot:

LUCKY ELEPHANT.
PLEASE RETURN.

Nita laughed. "Well, small elephant, if Sara has sent you to look after me, you'd better make sure you do. And I'd better get you home safely too."

Nita showed the wooden elephant to the others on the bike trip. He was not quite sure he enjoyed being laughed about, but, young or old, they seemed happy to have him join the expedition.

"An Indian elephant! What a great mascot, Nita," said Danny, the bike ride leader.

He felt relieved. Sometimes, during the long flight, Nita had looked troubled. He knew she was a good cyclist, but she was only just old enough for the bike ride. Maybe he shouldn't have agreed to let her come? Now he saw that her lively smile was back again, and all was well.

Danny glanced at his schedule, and went to check on the other cyclists. It was his job to keep them all safe and happy.

Nita thought, then took the long scarlet braid from her hair kit, and wound it across and around the small elephant's stout wooden belly, so that he dangled securely from a strong loop. It was wobbly, but she was sure it was better than being stuffed in that dark, uncomfortable bag.

"Time to see India, little one!" she said, as the tour bus arrived. It was going to take them all the way to the start of the ride, high in the hills.

The bus was not like any the small elephant had seen from Sara's window. It was as bright as a rainbow, and covered with garlands and jangling beads.

Ram, the driver, had a bushy black beard and wore a turban. He had brought his younger brother along to help with the driving. As the group gathered round, the two men began loading luggage onto the roof. When Danny had checked his lists, everyone climbed aboard.

As Nita got inside, Ram's eyes twinkled. He pointed to a front seat. "You'll get the best views from there, young lady," he told her. "Danny will sit nearby, so we can both tell you what to watch out for."

Nita wanted to see everything, so she sat where he suggested. As she got her camera from her bag, Ram spotted the small wooden elephant, and held out his hand. Hesitantly, Nita handed the elephant over.

"It seems to me that your little friend should have a good view too," Ram said, as he hung the small elephant inside the windscreen.

Ram's brother checked the doors were shut, then settled on one of the other seats, so he could doze and rest once the bus was on its way.

"Here we go!" Ram cried. The engine coughed and rattled into life. Ram tested the horn, and the bus set off, following the long road to the northern hills.

The small elephant twirled and turned on his scarlet braid, alarmed by his first glimpses of the road speeding past.

Buses, vans and crowded cars rushed by on all sides, hooting and tooting. Scooters and cycle-rickshaws and bikes darted across their path. Ram shouted violent warnings, shaking his head, but did not slow down.

Gradually, as the bus reached the edge of town,

the small elephant saw the road widen. Trucks and lorries and limousines sped along the centre lanes, leaving the edge of the road to a tangle of rusty vehicles, buffalo carts, and pushbikes weighed down with bundles of goods. Occasional ambling cattle wandered across the road, holding up everything.

Each time Ram pulled to a stop, children crowded round the bus, holding up drinks, postcards and souvenirs. Hollow-eyed beggars, wrapped in rags, pushed forward too, clustering around the travellers and asking for money.

At one stop, Ram's brother stretched, blinked himself awake, and paced about outside, drinking cans of Coke. When the bus set off again, he was at the wheel, but the ever-watchful Ram barely dozed.

Night came. Ram sang under his breath, a gentle lilting tune that made the small elephant feel at peace. Now and then, as he swung backwards and forwards, he caught the reflection in the windscreen, and saw Nita and the others asleep in their seats.

The bus left the plain, and fewer cars flashed past. As the road went up into the hills, the small elephant knew he had never seen such darkness. A wild, earthy smell filled the night air, and crept through the bus windows. The moon floated in the sky, larger and more mysterious than ever.

As the dark sky paled to grey, the driver pulled to a halt and turned off the engine. The passengers stirred in their seats.

"Why have we stopped?"

"Wait. Watch. You'll see," Ram told them. "Get your cameras ready."

Within minutes, the sky was glowing pink. The small elephant saw a vast mountain ridge stretching across the whole horizon. The faraway peaks were tipped with light.

"The Himalayas," breathed Nita, eyes wide.

The Himalayas? thought the small elephant.

Ram smiled at the sight, and nodded. "That is so. The roof of the world."

That night, the little elephant stood on the table in the hostel. The shutters were closed against the cool hill air, but street noises crept in through the metal window-screens. He thought of Ram and his many-coloured bus, but they were gone, back to the big city. All that the small elephant could see of Nita was a bulging sleeping bag in a top bunk.

A crumpled biscuit wrapper beside him rustled and a new mouse pattered delicately across it, picking up leftover crumbs. She eyed the small elephant.

"Hello! You are the creature who dreams of the white palace, I think?" she asked prettily.
"I've heard news of you, passed on by squeak and whisker, though one shouldn't always trust travellers' tales." She tiptoed round him. "You're not in bad shape, small elephant.

A few scratches here and there."

"Excuse me, are you another relation?" the small elephant enquired, thinking of the mice he'd met so far.

"I'm a very distant great-great-niece, three times removed!" she smiled, whisking her tail fetchingly.

"Pleased to meet you," the small elephant said. "But why are you interested in me?"

"Maybe we are all interested in a journey," she said, "especially one with a wish in it. How has it been so far?"

"Good, but bumpy," he admitted.

"Hmmm. Things will probably get bumpier soon," she told him, licking her whiskers clean.

"Bumpier?" he echoed, alarmed.

"Silly elephant!" said the mouse. "Journeys have downs as well as ups. Don't you know that? Good Luck!" And she darted away into the darkness.

"Ups and downs?" the small elephant thought, and a memory of the faded, far-off room appeared in his mind.

Where were the other two elephants now? Were their wishes answered when they flew from that high-up window? And what about the lovely lost white palace? He longed to see it again, but such a wish seemed unimportant compared to the task ahead.

The small elephant thought of Sara catching him as he fell, and the silvery music of her flute. She had called him her lucky elephant, and given him to Nita. But how, wooden carving that he was, could he help when even the mice seemed to know more than he did?

*   *   *

As everyone finished breakfast the next morning, a truck stacked with bicycles rattled into the hostel yard. Two young men jumped out, wearing T-shirts and jeans, and started unloading.

"Make sure your bike is the right height," called Danny, as everyone hurried outside. "Forget about shiny paint. Go for the comfortable saddle, and check your pedals are OK. Devi and Dez will help you."

Danny himself checked that Nita's bike fitted. Immediately, she looped the small elephant safely onto her handlebars, where he swayed gently on his red braid as she circled around in the sunshine, ringing her bell.

"Now, this ride is only a practice," called Danny, "but you'll need to take care."

He led the bikes off around the quieter streets of town, away from the frantic traffic. Even so, dogs dashed at their wheels, scooters puttered past them, and delivery trucks and vans braked in their path. It was scary. Gradually, street by street, swerve by swerve, dip by slope, Nita and the others cycled more confidently.

"Glad you're with me, lucky elephant," Nita panted, as she steered round a pothole.

The small elephant was glad too, but he felt every bump of the ride. He wondered if that was what the mouse meant by warning him of bumpiness ahead.

It turned into a long day. No sooner had the cyclists got back, parked their bikes, and eaten their lunch when Danny reminded them they wouldn't be resting for long. That afternoon, they were going out on foot to explore the old town.

Later that night, as everyone slept, the small elephant stood ready on Nita's pack. The cyclists were setting off at dawn, so that they could ride in the cool of the morning.

His mind was still full of the things he'd seen on the walk — the heaped vegetables and spices spread out in the market, the flamboyant silks and cloths in the bazaar, and the carpets like woven flower gardens.

As afternoon turned to evening, they had paused at stalls where pans of food sizzled over fierce flames, and where the buzz from Internet cafes and juice bars spilled out onto the pavements and squares.

The small elephant thought of the crowds enjoying themselves on the streets, flooding into the cinema, gossiping outside the ever-open shops, pausing at the temples, mosques, churches and shrines.

What he most remembered were elegant puppets acting out some ancient tale against a painted screen, while a storyteller sang out their great story.

"What is my story?" the small elephant wondered. *"What is my tale?"*

At that moment, he sensed that something was outside the window. For a second he was happy. It would be nice to tell a mouse about all he had seen. Then a long thin shape rose up against the window.

"Ssst! Ssst!" A snake was staring through the shutters, flickering its tongue. *"Huh! So you are the thing I've heard about,"* it sneered. *"The lucky elephant! You must have a high opinion of yourself, log-face. Whoever heard of a lump of wood helping anyone? As for wishing to see a pretty white palace? You might as well wish for castles in the air, you fool!"* The snake laughed nastily and slid away.

The trickle of words turned into doubt in the elephant's mind. What did he think he was doing here, so far from that forgotten room? Then Nita shifted in her sleep and the small elephant remembered. No matter what the snake said, no matter how frightened he grew, Sara had sent him on this journey to help Nita, and he would if he could.

The following morning was the start of the real bike ride, so there were plenty of photographs. Nita fastened the small elephant onto her handlebars, and the riders set off along the busy streets. After an hour, Danny signalled and they all turned off the main road, away from the riot of traffic.

It was quieter, but it was now that the difficult bit began. Over the coming days, the route would loop down and up, down and around and down the foothills of the great mountains. The cyclists were heading east, towards the rising sun and the banks of a great river that was now far, far beyond their sight.

Nita found it exhilarating, as she freewheeled down dips, steered around uneven curves, then pedalled hard up the next steep slope. Screeches and shouts passed along the line of riders.

"Look out! Careful! Watch out for that hole!" they called. The ride was tough work, and the quiet road was often rutted and uneven.

The small elephant heard Nita panting as she pushed harder and harder, and the bike sped forwards. Swinging about on the handlebars, he felt each rattle of the bike's frame. But he also saw shafts of sun lighting up the larches and evergreens, and small streams rushing down the valleys, still full of water from the last monsoon. On and on they went.

Each evening, the cyclists stayed at a different hostel. As moths and flies flew against the screens, trying to reach the glowing lamps within, the small elephant would watch everyone scribbling down that day's distance in their diaries. They chatted about families and sponsors, and joked with Devi and Dez, the truck drivers, who drove all the heavy luggage from one hostel to the next, and made sure there was an evening meal.

On the fourth day, as everyone sped along, Danny yelled out, and waved furiously. "Slow! Slow! Bad road ahead!"

The riders braked, almost colliding, and Nita shot

into a grassy verge before she could stop. The small elephant saw the trees rushing towards them, and at the last moment, Nita managed to topple the bike into the soft earth. Danny ran towards her.

"Silly girl," she heard someone say. "Going too fast."

"We were all going fast," another voice said.

"It's all right. I'm not really hurt," Nita said loudly, trying to laugh it off. She was badly grazed, nothing worse, but it took some time to fix her front tyre. Most of the cyclists were pleased to dawdle among the trees, but there were one or two sour faces.

"Probably they were the ones who braked badly in the first place," Danny whispered to Nita. "Don't worry."

That night, the small elephant heard Nita muttering in her sleep and felt anxious.

It wasn't long before he saw something slither up to the window and stare in. "Sssst! Sssst! Shouldn't you be doing something?"  *hissed the snake as it coiled and writhed in the moonlight.*

"I do. I bring her luck," the small elephant insisted.

"Didn't do very well with the luck today, did you? Maybe it was you that tangled up her steering, twig-head. Call yourself

lucky? Your head must be full of woodworm. Sssssssst!" it spat. "Just who do you think you are?"

The snake slithered off, and the night became long and empty. The small elephant hoped a friendly mouse might visit, but none did. Gradually, Nita drifted into silent sleep.

"Things could be worse," the small elephant told himself, "and tomorrow is another day. Maybe I will be better with my luck tomorrow."

At breakfast, everyone was yawning and rubbing sore legs and shoulders. Nita had dark rings under her eyes. Nobody spoke. But once they got on their bikes, everyone felt better. Laughing and joking, they had a wonderful ride.

After a picnic lunch, Danny led them down a path, where a river had cut its way between the rocks. The wooden elephant, still tied to the bike, watched Nita go further and further down, until she stood on a narrow bridge, watching the water plunge down to the valley below. Spray shone like a rainbow around her, and she seemed as small as he was, and a very long way away.

The path back up was steep, so they rested on the river bank, where the water had carved out a shallow pool. Nita flung off her shoes, and stepped out onto the rocks. More warily, a couple of others followed her. Nita dabbled her toes in the water, and hopped from one stone to another, as happy as a bird. Soon, she was dancing here and there, splashing about and shrieking with joy, until everyone was laughing with her.

Suddenly, with a cry, Nita slipped right in, drenching the people nearest to her. Danny dashed forward, and helped her out, dripping.

The group crowded round, so the small elephant did not know what was happening. *Nita,* he thought helplessly, *Nita!* Only when he saw them all start back up the path through the trees did he stop worrying.

Nita was wet through, and rather shaken, though she was trying to laugh it off. Most of the others were laughing with her, but there were a couple of cross faces.

"Silly girl! If she'd really hurt herself, it would have ruined our ride," one commented loudly.

"Might have hurt someone else, too!"

"A mistake to let someone so young come along," grumbled the first.

As Nita set off on her bike again, the small elephant could see she was upset. "My stupid fault," she muttered under her breath, as she pushed angrily at the pedals.

"Don't worry about them, dear. These things happen," one of the cyclists told her, with a wide smile across her wrinkled face. "It was a pleasure to see you having fun! Almost joined you myself."

"Thanks!" Nita mumbled, keeping her head down.

* * *

That evening, the small elephant saw Nita sitting list-lessly. She said she was too tired to eat.

"You must have something," Danny told her. "You need the energy." Nita nodded, but only ate one mouthful.

After supper, Danny got out a mouth organ, and began to play a tune. Nita gave a start, because it was a tune that Sara sometimes played. All at once, she really missed her home, and she missed Mum and Sara and Nanji. Nita snatched up the small elephant, turned away and hurried to her bed. She curled up in the sleeping bag, and shut her eyes tight. It was so unfair. She was only having fun in that pool!

Nita was fed up with being the youngest. She was fed up with trying to be best, and trying to be nice. She was fed up with bumping into people and having them bump into her. Most of all, she was fed up with trying to do this wretched bike ride. She held the small elephant close, feeling rather foolish, considering how old she was, but she was too upset to care.

Gradually, as Nita held him tight between her warm palms, she smelt a scent that took her heart straight home. It was Nanji's lovely oil, the oil she'd used to clean the carved wooden elephant.

"Tell me," the small elephant seemed to say to her. "Tell me what's wrong."

"I must do this ride. I must."

"Why?"

"For my daddy," she sighed. "He taught me to ride long ago, before Sara was born. We'd get up really early, and go out cycling around the streets and across the parks. Just the two of us, our own special time..."

"And?" came the question.

Nita hesitated. She stroked the small elephant's smooth forehead, and the round curve of the carved body and even the sticking-up corner of label on his foot. She thought of the small elephant standing on Nanji's golden silk cloth, among the glowing diva lights.

"And he told me that one day he'd take me to India, and we'd cycle side by side."

"So?" the small elephant seemed to say. "It is very sad that he can't be here. But it seems to me that your daddy would be proud and happy that you are here, and he would wish you to be happy, too."

"But, but..."

"Would it have been better not to have done this? Not to have had a dream at all?"

"No," Nita murmured.

"Then sleep, Nita. Sleep."

The small elephant lay in her hands, against the pillow. He did not care when strange voices hissed in the darkness outside, or called him names. The small elephant was not sure where the words he had used tonight had come from, but he was glad Nita had heard them.

*   *   *

Later, when Danny peeped in to check the girl was all right, he found her clutching the wooden elephant tightly.

"Nothing like a lucky mascot when you need one," he murmured.

Next day, Nita was laughing and singing again, cheering everyone else up. She would do it. She would get there, no matter what. She would finish the bike ride!

"Let's go, everyone!" she called, intending to keep up with Danny as long as she could. Even yesterday's sour faces were smiling again today.

As they cycled on, the forest turned into green-tea terraces, then into fields dotted with villages of flat-roofed houses, and criss-crossed by ditches where long-necked birds dived for fish and snakes.

As the bike riders got closer to the city, the road filled with ramshackle lorries and souvenir sellers. Groups of travellers surged along the highway, towards the holy river and the festival. The days and nights were noisier.

At last, the twelfth and final day of the bike ride came. One by one, the cyclists freewheeled into the grounds of a comfortable hostel, where staff were waiting to greet them. They had done it! They had finished the long journey. All that was left was two days of sightseeing, then home.

"Yeeeehaaa!" yelled Nita as she swept in through the gate, arms aloft. She could hardly believe she had made the distance. "Well done, you," she muttered, untying the little elephant.

Then she found herself smothered in enthusiastic hugs.

"Well done, Nita," everyone was saying. "You were fantastic. It was so nice to have you with us. You did really well, pet!"

"You too! You too! " Nita answered, grinning at all the smiling faces. "It was great, wasn't it?"

"Well done, all of you!" cried Danny.

"Well done, Danny!" they shouted back.

Now the bike riders could go home, their sponsorship forms victoriously stamped.

Even Devi and Dez, arriving with the truck of luggage, were full of smiles. Tomorrow, they'd be taking the hired bikes back, but tonight there was the festival to enjoy.

Nita tied the small elephant onto her shoulder bag, and joined the others. Danny led them to the old part of the city, thronged with eager travellers. Temples and shrines and ornate towers clustered at the edge of the holy river, which swirled against the stone ghats, and surged past the stepped embankments where hundreds of pilgrims clustered.

Danny took them towards a holy man draped in orange robes, who was waiting on the wide steps, close to the water. The man's brown eyes twinkled, and his white hair and beard trailed about him. Two young boys accompanied the holy man. They had shaven heads and solemn eyes, and carried garlands of yellow marigolds. The holy man and Danny bowed, greeting each other with pleasure.

"So, you have arrived at the end of another trip, my friend," the holy man said, smiled around at everyone. "Certainly, it is a cause for happiness, a moment for true thanks for you all."

As the young apprentices placed the bright garlands around every neck, the holy man marked every forehead with vermilion powder and gave each traveller a lighted diva lamp. Then, reaching into a basket, he scattered clouds of petals on the river, muttering many words of prayer.

One by one, the travellers set their flickering lamps on the sacred water. The shining divas circled around each other, then, like ribbons of light, floated away with the mighty river. The small elephant thought he had never seen anything so lovely, except for his lost white palace.

"Now for the fireworks," said Danny.

This time they followed the crowds, surging into a big square. As they arrived, the first fireworks went up, scattering a dazzle of stars across the sky, and the music began. Navarartri – The Festival of the Ninth Night – had arrived.

Explosions lit the darkness. Fireworks flowered with crackles and bangs, or fell like molten silver fountains from the sky. The smell of the city was mixed with the whiff of acrid smoke. The small elephant found it all alarming and wonderful, but then, as Nita whirled round to see more, he was filled with terror.

Three grimacing figures, huger than houses, loomed at the other side of the square. They were the effigies of the Demon Ravanna and his two demon sons, who had battled against the good Lord Rama, and failed. Even now, their faces glittered with wickedness. Broken wood and crumpled boards were stacked in heaps around their feet.

As the frantic music whirled, the small elephant saw tongues of flame leap from the bonfires and lick around the three demons. Soon they were captured in cages of flame. For a moment, they swayed menacingly in the blaze. Then they fell with a roar, destroyed for another year. Everyone cheered, and a cacophony of drums beat out in triumph.

The Monkey King Hanuman had overcome the demon hordes! The victorious Lord Rama could reclaim his dear wife Sita and everyone would be happy again! Firecrackers exploded, rockets filled the night with ripples of brightness and the heavens lit up above the small elephant's head. A surprising idea came into his mind. *The journey! It is almost over*, he thought. *I will be back soon, and I will hear Sara's flute again.*

There was one last day of weary travelling, when the crowded train rattled across the endless plain, and dust blew in through the barred windows. The small elephant saw relief on everyone's faces as the great city came into view.

There would be no more hard bunks in plain hostels. Tonight they were staying in a luxurious hotel, and tomorrow there was only one important sightseeing trip to make before they went to the airport.

As soon as Nita reached her hotel room, she spread her things out, scribbled her last postcards and showered so her hair was spiky and glossy again.

Dressed and clean, Nita picked up the carved figure. She took a damp tissue and wiped the dust from the carved hide. "Don't know what I'd have done without you, small elephant," she said. "Thank you!"

Then she went to the hotel lounge and sank gratefully into one of the armchairs. She perched the small elephant on its wide arm, but soon she was up again, darting about, exchanging addresses and memories of the trip with the others. Now they were all such friends.

The small elephant, left on the chair arm, felt someone staring at him. It was a boy who leant against a pillar, quietly listening to all that went on. He was about the same age as Sara, but with pale blond hair and intense blue eyes. He had fixed them on the little wooden animal.

Nita, circling the crowd of people, noticed the blond boy and grinned at him. "Hi!" she said. "Having a good time?"

At that moment, a tall man — a father or an uncle, perhaps — came up behind the boy. The man had dark curly hair, grizzled with grey.

"All right, Jack? Ready for dinner?" he said.

The boy's face grew sullen and his eyes cold. He clenched his jaw and ignored the man. A shadow passed over the man's face and he went on to the restaurant alone. The small elephant saw the boy smile with satisfaction.

It was late by the time Nita got back to her room from the party. As she snuggled down under the smooth sheets, not bothering to move her things, something fluttered down onto the rug. It was a travel brochure.

The small elephant looked once, then twice and felt as if something magical had happened. There before him was a picture of his wish, his dream, his beloved white palace. All night he gazed at it, wondering what this meant.

At five the next morning he heard a knocking at the door.

"Hurry up, Nita. You'll be late!" someone called. "Are you awake? The coach is here."

Nita sat up in bed, blinking and yawning. She switched on the light, and struggled to her feet.

"Yes, I am," she mumbled, untruthfully. "Ready soon, OK?"

Half asleep, she grabbed her scattered belongings and stuffed them into her big rucksack. She could hear thumps and bumps in the corridor as the others carried their luggage to the coach. Today would be one long last day, sightseeing. Then, soon after midnight, she would be on the plane home.

With her main luggage packed, Nita snatched up her last bits and pieces – notebook, wallet, passport and tickets, travel brochures – and thrust them all in her shoulder bag. She seized the small elephant, looping his red braid over a buckle on her bag.

Danny knocked at Nita's door. She opened it.

"Ready? Need a hand?" he asked.

"Please," Nita said.

Danny hoisted her big rucksack on his shoulder and shooed Nita out of the room. She grabbed at her bag, tugging it free of the bedclothes, and they hurtled along the hotel corridor, out to where the coach stood, engine grumbling.

Alone, under the bed, the small elephant heard the coach pulling away. He had been left behind. The red braid was still wound around his carved belly, but its two torn, worn ends lay frayed and useless on the floor. The light had been switched off. Now, in the darkness, the small elephant thought he saw the fiery faces of those three terrible demons. They were laughing at him, mocking his vain wishes and the vanished dream of a white palace.

"Mouse, mouse?" called the small elephant, as a thin furry creature scampered and skated across the polished bedroom floor.

The mouse slid to a stop, panting. "Hello! Have they gone?" he asked. "Don't worry. Nobody stays here long. You'll be moving soon, you know."

"How?"

"Simple. Someone will sweep you up. Then you'll be Lost Property, won't you?" the mouse answered, as he nibbled away some stray red threads for its nest.

"But I'm not Lost — I'm Left Behind," said the small elephant.

"Lost Property. Left Behind. Sounds the same to me. Thanks for the threads, by the way," said the mouse, scrabbling away under the door.

The small elephant lay there, thinking of Nita and Sara and the picture of the lost white palace.

JACK

Not long after, a cleaner tugged the sheets off Nita's empty bed and scooped up the forgotten elephant. She stuffed it into her cleaning trolley, then hurried off to strip the bed next door.

Jack came sidling down the corridor, taking the long way down to breakfast on purpose. Angus would be waiting, but so what? Jack hadn't wanted to come on this trip. He hadn't wanted his mum to stay at home, working on her so-important project, either. Wasn't he important? Didn't he matter?

Mum had said she was sorry, over and over, but that he should go. She told him that all the arrangements had been made at his school. Did he care? No! Then she said that the trip would give him time to get to know Angus. Get to know Angus? Was that the plan? Ha! As soon as Jack met Angus, he'd made a decision. He would never, ever, ever speak to this man

It had worked fine at home. Jack had kept his mouth shut and his eyes blank, and never said a word to Angus. He was determined this trip to India wouldn't break him either. Why should he make friends? If he started to like him, the man would disappear, like his father and the others had done.

As Jack mooched down the corridor, he spotted the wooden elephant among the soaps and shampoos on the cleaning trolley. Quickly, he reached out and slipped it onto his pocket.

It wasn't really stealing. He was just looking after it. Far better for it than being dumped in a stinky lost

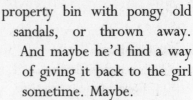

property bin with pongy old sandals, or thrown away. And maybe he'd find a way of giving it back to the girl sometime. Maybe.

Jack smiled. He marched down to breakfast and plonked the wooden animal on the table. He glared at Angus and ate, as ever, in carefully created silence.

"Listen, Jack," Angus said, putting down his empty cup. "I know you don't like me, and that you don't want to talk to me. It's a shame. I'm sorry Rosie made you come."

The boy gave a slight shrug, and carried on peeling an orange.

"But you have to understand that these next weeks will be tough. We'll be travelling to too many places in too little time. If I don't get my photographs, this assignment will be ruined. I'm not taking holiday snaps, I'm trying to tell a story. OK?"

Jack didn't answer. Not a word, not a breath.

"All I ask is that you don't mess it up," sighed Angus, crumpling his napkin. "We'll be leaving about eleven."

Mum was always spending money on him. She'd given him a brand-new digital camera, just so he'd feel part of Angus's trip. Jack pushed the brand-new camera into his brand-new bag, and was ready. He didn't want Angus to think he was a wimp who couldn't look after himself.

Then he picked up the wooden elephant. Now he had a moment, he could see that the thing was really quite old. The red threads were faded and sun-bleached. Perhaps that girl had hung the carving on her bicycle for luck.

He tipped it this way and that. The small elephant had a shy, pleasant face that made Jack feel amused. And there, on one foot, was all that was left of a grubby label:

PLEASE RETURN.

So, the girl *did* want the thing back. Jack stood there, studying the carved creature. Then he stuffed it in his pocket again, and lugged his bags downstairs to the hotel office.

"Yes? Can I help you?" said a young woman in a bright pink suit.

"Maybe. I saw a girl here last night." Jack thought of the conversation he'd overheard in the lounge. "Nita. She was with the charity bike ride. Can you tell me how to get in touch with her?"

"Do you mean the girl with the spiky hair?" she smiled.

Jack blushed, and flicked his own hair out of his eyes. Did the woman think he had a crush on Nita?

"Yes, that girl," he muttered. "I wanted to ask her about the trip."

"Sorry," the receptionist told him briskly. "I can't give you any personal information."

"Please, there must be some way?" Jack put on his most charming smile, the one that made him look like his father; the smile he hated. It worked.

She smiled back, checked a list and scribbled something down. "I can give you the name of the organizers. They may be able to help."

"Thanks." Jack slipped the paper into his pocket, next to the carved animal. He'd work out what to do about it later.

"Come on," he said to the small elephant as he lifted his travel bags. "Let's go and find that man."

Angus was right about the travelling, Jack discovered. For several days, their lives were a kaleidoscope of taxis and cars, planes, buses and trucks. Afterwards, it was only the important times that Jack remembered.

As a small plane flew them, on one of the days, in to land at a local airport, Jack saw, below him, the intense blue of the ocean and long sandy beaches fringed by palm trees, with huts and hotels along the edge of the water. He nearly tugged at Angus's sleeve in his excitement, but remembered in time, and clenched his fist. Anyway, Angus had work to do, and they might not even make it to the beach.

"Who's that?" whispered one mouse to another, as Jack and Angus lay dozing in yet another hotel room. Pale threads of sunlight shone through the bamboo blinds.

"It's a wooden elephant. I heard that he's come to see a white palace," the second mouse replied.

"Is that so?"

The two mice clustered around the third elephant, running their tiny paws over his wooden body.

"What do you know about that white palace, child?" said the first mouse.

"I only know it was beautiful," said the small elephant.

"And what do you know about yourself?" said the second.

"I'm an elephant, that's what I am," he answered, boldly. He was surprised to hear how much braver he sounded than in that half-forgotten room. "A lucky elephant."

"But what is an elephant, child?" they teased, gently patting his carved trunk. "Is it a long trunk or huge ears or four strong legs? Is it ivory tusks or a wrinkled hide?"

"I'm sorry. I don't know," he said, hesitantly.

"Then the wheel of life will take you onwards. You still have plenty to learn, little one, both you and the boy you travel with."

Jack slung the wooden elephant, knotted around with string, nonchalantly over his shoulder, and followed

Angus and his camera kit out of the hotel.

Angus strode along streets crammed with noisy bars and garish signs, past the spicy scent of food stalls, past juice-carts laden with oranges, limes and mangoes. Tourists in smart shades crowded the souvenir shops, haggling and gabbling.

Eventually, Angus turned into a quieter road of shuttered houses with flaking pink plaster, where purple flowers clambered over the rooftiles. They walked towards an ancient wall with a huge gateway. Two wooden gates, studded with iron and warped with age, stood open.

Angus and Jack went through the cool shadow of the archway into a wide mud-paved courtyard. A vast stone trough filled with water stood in the centre, and there was a smell of hay and animal dung. On one side of the square stood an enormous stableblock.

A handsome man in a long linen shirt ran out to greet them. "Namaste! Hello, Angus! So good to see you again."

"Namaste, Ranjit! Good to see you too," Angus replied, bowing in return.

"You must be Rosie's son?" Ranjit said, with a welcoming smile, but Jack nodded abruptly. Taken aback by the boy's rudeness, Ranjit turned to Angus. "You'll have to hurry. They're preparing Princess now." He gestured across to the stable. "She has to be at work soon."

"Thanks, Ranjit," Angus said, unstrapping his camera

bag. "We're meeting for that meal later? Great!"

At that moment, the small elephant saw something enormous amble from the darkness of the stables. Even with all his dreams and wishes, this was something he had not imagined. In the centre of the yard was … was … was… ? Did he know?

Yes, he did know. This was a true, living elephant. Not a hard carved wooden elephant, but something with an enormous body that swayed, and a long trunk that curled and coiled and enormous painted ears that flapped in the sun. Her mighty feet, with brightly coloured toenails, raised clouds of dust as she walked.

The small elephant would have cheered if he could, for this living elephant was not wreathed in silence like that solid pair on the long-ago shelf. This elephant grunted and snuffled and coughed and made loud noises in front and behind. She was real and alive.

Her bright greedy eyes were fixed on the bundles of sugarcane her wrinkled mahout was using to entice her out into the courtyard. The man was not much heavier than Jack, but strong and wiry.

"Meet Princess," said Ranjit.

At the mahout's command, Princess coiled her strong grey trunk. As he placed his sandalled foot on it, she raised him up and over the dome of her head, to a small cloth saddle-pad. Muttering lovingly, the mahout took Princess round the yard, easing the itches between her shoulder blades with the handle of his metal-pronged ankush. Several young men hovered

around, waiting to help with her final preparations. Princess slowly flapped her flower-patterned ears, showing off for the camera lens.

Angus circled around, taking pictures from all angles. Jack moved closer, lifting his own camera. Hanging at his side, the small wooden elephant gazed at the marvellous being, delighted.

As Princess drew level, she paused, studying Jack and then the small elephant with long-lashed, intelligent eyes. She ran the tip of her long trunk enquiringly over the carving, and her pink mouth gaped in a kind of grin.

The mahout's face broke into an amused smile too. "What's this, boy? You have your own elephant already?" he joked.

Jack blushed and stepped back, out of reach of the tickling trunk. The mahout took Princess a few more paces, then slid down, tucking the hook of his ankush in the elephant's neck rope.

At his command, Princess knelt, and three assistants brought out a thickly padded blanket to protect her back. Once the protection was strapped into place, they covered it with an embroidered cloth, unfolding the shimmering, sequinned flaps down both her sides.

Finally, they brought out what seemed to Jack to be a low, upside-down table. As it was hauled up onto Princess's back, secured and stuffed with padded cushions, Jack saw that it was a howdah, for carrying passengers. As his assistants worked, the mahout gave orders, checking every piece of the elephant's harness until he was satisfied.

All the time, Angus was taking his pictures. Once Princess was dressed, one of the assistants spread out a bucketful of rice, fruit and coconuts, which she crunched greedily.

"Angus, we must let them go," Ranjit said, pointing at his watch. Angus called his thanks to the mahout. "Magnificent," he said. "She'll impress the tourists."

"You should see her on festival days," Ranjit said, "when we put on her headdress. Then she looks like a royal elephant indeed. Do you want to ride down to the temple?"

"No, thanks. We'll follow you," Angus replied, to Jack's disappointment.

The mahout gave a shout, and Princess moved off through the arched gateway. Jack heard cries of delight as the glittering elephant plodded off down the road.

The assistants ran alongside. One was bowed under a sack of food to keep Princess happily fed. Another was weighed down by a leather money satchel. The third boy, dressed in bright silk, beat a drum and sang out to attract the crowd as they processed towards the temple. Angus saw Jack's smile of admiration.

"She looks like a princess," Angus told him, "but the ones that get rich are her wealthy owners. The mahout and his men just get enough to live on."

Ranjit nodded. "That's true. She'll be working for hours now. At least Princess is well looked after, not like some of the poor beasts I've seen."

Jack hated hearing about elephants being badly treated. He clenched his hand around the small wooden elephant and twisted away from the comforting hand Angus placed on his shoulder.

"Elephants like Princess are part of my story," said Angus, setting off down the street at a run. "Come on. We have to get to the temple now."

By the time Angus and Jack reached the temple forecourt, Princess was lined up with several other magnificent elephants, each with their own mahout and minders. As visitors scrambled and struggled up into her howdah, Angus took more photographs.

Jack watched Princess plodding up the long slope towards the upper temple yard, past the carvings and statues. Two more elephants passed her, coming back with their loads of goggling tourists. The sun blazed down, making the sequinned trappings glitter. The mighty creatures moved on, endlessly picking up people and setting down people. There were several hours to go before their work was ended.

Jack was fascinated by the procession of elephants, and by the way the elephant men worked the crowds. Jack was fascinated by Angus at work too, though he would not show it. The man was careful in the way he photographed. He really cared about what he was doing.

Jack felt a second of grudging respect, and paused. He must remember not to give this man the satisfaction of a single word. Did he want to talk to Angus? No way! Never, ever. He curled his lip. But as he chose not to speak, Jack somehow felt as if he had lost the power to leave his path of silence, as if silence was now choosing him. Angrily, as they left the temple, he swung his wooden elephant about.

"I'll be like you, elephant," he muttered in his head. "Seeing nothing, feeling nothing. Never getting hurt."

"Mouse, mouse!" called the small elephant, as a tiny creature scurried past, taking wisps of hay to her nest. "Please? What do I look like? Do I have any patterns on my sides?"

"Wait a moment," the mouse said, twitching her nose thoughtfully. She disappeared with the hay, and returned with a shard of broken mirror.

"See for yourself," she said, holding the mirror at an angle, and moving slowly round the wooden figure.

"Yes," said the small elephant, peering hard. "I see."

He saw himself — his round rump and the faint pattern of dots that decorated his sides, his round belly looped with Jack's string, his wide ears, his trunk, his tiny elephant eyes and his curved smile.

"So that's who I am. That is

myself!" he thought, regarding his figure with a touch of admiration. *"Thank you, mouse."*

When the mouse had gone, the third elephant thought of the beautiful Princess. The mahout and his men loved her. The raucous crowds loved to look at her. But how long did an Indian elephant, even if she was a Princess, last on the crowded city streets? He was grateful for his unfeeling wooden hide.

After another long journey, Jack sat wooden-faced in the rear of the jeep. They were on the way to Angus's next assignment. Jack clutched the small elephant as the vehicle bumped along the dirt roads of the wildlife reserve. Angus and his driver chatted in the front.

At last, Angus turned to Jack. "That's where we're going," he pointed. "Over there. Sanctuary Lodge."

The rough road led around a big lake edged with muddied drinking places. Dark birds rose like flapping rags, and circled overhead. The jeep came to a stop outside a long, low bungalow sheltered by huge trees. Scarlet flowers and creepers flowed over the veranda roof. Peacocks strutted up and down, fanning their tails and screeching. Around the lake, under another clump of trees, were a few thatched-roof holiday lodges.

A slender woman with a plait of dark hair waited on the veranda steps, shading her eyes. As soon as she recognized Angus, she waved both arms.

"Hello, Kal!" Angus called, beaming, as he gathered up his luggage.

Jack struggled out of the jeep, rubbing his cramped legs. Flights, hotels and endless journeys. He couldn't believe how big this country was, or the way that Angus charged about in it.

"Come inside. There's cool drinks ready," Kal said. "Is this the boy you told us about?" she asked, smiling at Jack. "You're welcome."

How had Angus had described him, Jack wondered. A spoilt brat? Nothing but bother? A nuisance? He tensed his shoulders defiantly and swung the wooden elephant backwards and forwards.

"Bring your things through here, Jack," Kal said, with an easy smile, showing him to a large, comfortable bedroom. "This is yours. You can come here whenever you want a bit of time to yourself. It's not always fun being with grown-ups, especially when they're busy."

Jack almost thanked her. The room felt good to him. It wasn't blank and tidy like the hotels they'd stayed in. Nor was it tight with tension, like home had been. He smiled, dumped down his things and opened the shutters. Just beyond the mosquito screen, a family of monkeys played and squabbled among the overhanging branches of the sheltering trees. Further off, a herd of spotted deer, half-hidden by the long grass, ran across his view.

"It's great here," Jack breathed, setting the wooden elephant on the window sill. He lay on the bed and closed his eyes.

*   *   *

It was hours later when Jack woke. He could hear a generator humming and birds calling. He heard voices, too. Silently, he padded across the polished wooden floors of the lodge, until he reached the office.

Kal, Angus and another man were huddled around a computer screen. The man wore dusty trek boots, and a rifle and a belt of shot lay on the table at his side. Jack edged forward, listening.

They seemed to be studying lists of data. "You can see by the records that the herd figures are down," the man said.

"I can't believe it, Hari. Your oldest male elephant!" Angus exclaimed. "I photographed that bull on my last visit."

"Poachers got him just before the monsoon came. They were after his tusks, of course. It was terrible." Hari's voice was hollow, his dark eyes desolate.

"A bloody waste!" spat Angus.

"It's worse than that," said Kal. "We've only got two grown bull elephants in the Sanctuary now. The rest of the young males won't be fathers for years yet."

"We're already struggling to keep the numbers level," Hari added. "We've put out a request to see if we can find any others."

"But will the poacher gangs keep away from them if you do?" Angus snapped, angrily.

"We have to keep trying, Angus," Hari said.

❧ 77 ❧

Just then, Kal glanced up from the screen and saw Jack. Angus and Hari put on jokey, friendly faces, but Kal eyed Jack closely, as if she knew he'd heard their desperation.

"You must have been tired, Jack. You slept for ages," she said.

Just then, the kitchen door opened, and Sanctuary Lodge filled with the rattle of dishes and delicious smells. "But you woke in time for food, boy!" Kal grinned. "Let's wash, and then we can eat. I'm starving."

Later, as the sun was dropping in the sky, Kal came over to Jack.

"Angus and Hari will be chatting for ages," she said. "Want to see something wonderful instead?"

Jack hesitated, then he gave the slightest nod.

Kal and Jack set off around the lake to a rough bamboo hide, sheltered by some bushes.

"Wait!" she said. "Let me make sure there's nothing nasty inside, first." She checked the walls, floor and ceiling, and looked under the benches. Then she led the way in. The hide gave a wonderful view of the lake, and all the animals' drinking places. The setting sun was painting the sky gold.

Kal showed Jack her binoculars. "Use them if you want," she said, and settled back comfortably.

Jack sat there, heart beating, his hand tensed around the small elephant. He was really excited, but he must remember not to say a word to Kal, no matter how kind she was. If he spoke to Kal or to Hari or anyone, he might give in and speak to Angus. But Kal just smiled. She didn't seem to mind whether he talked to her or not.

The small wooden elephant felt Jack squeezing him so tightly that he was sure he'd break. Then the boy relaxed. As a herd of elephants approached the lake, Jack reached out for the binoculars.

The small elephant watched too. He saw the sturdy bodies, the tall wise foreheads, and the flapping ears that were shaped like India herself. Like one large family — babies, young ones, mothers and grandmothers — the elephants moved into the water, ripples circling out around them. They lifted streams of shining water into their mouths, washing away the thirst of the day. They played gently and easily, swishing the water and wading into the deeper pools, until they had had enough. The small wooden elephant stared at their freedom, and felt something like envy. At last the herd wandered off, giving a few sad calls that echoed across the trampled grass, as if they were calling to the ghosts of their herd.

When night came, a rather portly mouse clambered up the bedpost and pottered across the sill. He folded his paws and fixed his eyes firmly on the wooden elephant.

"So, all is well, young one?" he said. "Your travels are good for you?"

The small elephant mused for a moment on all the richness he had seen so far. "Yes, thank you, my friend."

"And how about the boy? Are his travels good?"

The small elephant hesitated. "He says nothing."

The mouse raised his eyes to the ceiling in exasperation, and tutted. "Is he happy in his silence? Does he like his peace and quiet? Maybe someone should make him think about these things?"

"What can I do?" *said the third elephant.*

The mouse looked at him sternly. "Something is better than nothing, I would say. Watch out for the right moment. Good night."

Angus went out early with Hari next morning, letting Jack sleep. When they sat down for lunch, Hari was beaming. An email had arrived, saying that a young bull elephant was available in another state. It would take time to get him to the Sanctuary, and time to settle the newcomer among the other males, but it was hopeful news.

"Do you want to send any emails, Jack?" Kal asked. "Our connections aren't always reliable, so do get online while you can."

Jack glanced at Angus, who shrugged. "Go on, if you want to."

Kal took Jack along to the office, set up the computer, patted his shoulder calmly and left him to it.

Jack emailed his mum, telling her yet again that he was all right. She'd pick up his message when she checked her morning mail.

Then he hesitated, turning the wooden elephant over in his palm. He picked at the label. The little carving didn't truly belong to him. He paused, glanced at the details he'd been given back at the hotel, then typed them into the search engine. Soon the bike ride website came up on the screen. He clicked on the CONTACT icon, and wrote.

"Subject: IMPORTANT LOST PROPERTY. Message: Request! Please x 100 forward this message to NITA who was on the India bike ride." He checked the wall calendar and added the date he'd seen her at the hotel. "Dear Nita, I have found a WOODEN ELEPHANT. Get in touch if you want to. From Jack." For a moment, he grinned. It seemed ages since he'd chosen to do anything positive. Swiftly, he clicked SEND.

"See?" he told the small elephant who was standing by the mouse-mat. "If she wants you, she'll let me know." He felt better about taking the carved elephant now.

"Done?" said Kal, coming back in. "Good. Want to come and see Cook's parrot? He is one very rude bird!"

Together, they walked down the side veranda to where the cook sat, drinking his tea. A large green parrot sat on a perch beside him. As they approached, it sidled along the perch towards them, putting its head on one side in the friendliest way.

"Bog off!" it croaked.

They all burst out laughing. "It wasn't me who taught him to say that!" chuckled the cook. "That's a bad, bad bird! You're lucky you didn't come when I had my mynah bird – he was even worse!"

As the next day dawned, the small elephant watched Jack turning restlessly in his bed. Every so often, the boy muttered in his sleep.

A pair of identical mice pattered across the bedroom floor. They looked up as Jack mumbled to himself.

"So the boy can speak then, my sister?" one said.

"If he wants to, my sister," said the other.

"It can't be easy for that human bean of a child, being

dragged about all the time."

"No it can't!" the second sister said.

"And now he'll be on the move again! Here, there and back again. What do you say about it, small elephant? Is your journey easy?"

"Not easy," said the small elephant, "but it is often good."

"And the white palace?"

"Oh, that? I don't know," he told them, and he was surprised to find he had not thought about it for ages.

They were on their way again. For most of the journey, a small plane had flown them over ugly factory towns, across wide meandering rivers, over small villages among paddy fields and up long tree-lined ridges.

Now Jack was hunched up in a truck, bouncing along a forest road. His head was buzzing. He was angry with Angus. He hadn't wanted to leave Kal and Hari and the Sanctuary so quickly. *As soon as the man gets his pictures, off he goes again*, Jack thought bitterly.

Now they were travelling through thickly wooded hills. In places, the dense cover of green leaves gave way to stretches of empty ground, where logging teams had cleared the slopes below. Jack saw the empty ground turn into the terraces of tea plantations. As Angus took the truck around another bend, they saw an express train in the valley below. It flashed like a silver bullet along a gleaming track that ran through the remaining trees. To Jack's surprise, Angus swore.

"That damn railway cuts right across the migration tracks," he yelled to no one in particular. "Elephants don't know about rail safety. The damned trains kill them: young ones, mothers, babies. God, it's a horrible sight."

Jack stared at the floor of the truck. He wanted to speak, wanted to ask more, but still refused to let the words form in his mouth.

"That's what my work's about, Jack," Angus went on, grimly, as the truck crossed a metal girder bridge and entered another valley. "I'm not just rushing about for no reason. I'm trying to get information together, trying to tell people what's happening to these creatures before the only elephant kids like you will see is a blasted computer image."

Angus had calmed down by the time they came, eventually, to a part of the forest where leaves glistened on the branches and ferns filled the hollows. They turned up a narrow road and stopped in front of a large colonial bungalow, set on a ridge. A servant in a smart shirt and shorts hurried out to help them with their luggage.

Two young girls darted out onto the steps, giggling. A tall man with a handsome bearded face appeared behind them. Scooping a boisterous toddler onto his shoulder, he came down the steps towards the truck. His smiling wife stood in the doorway.

"Angus, my friend! You can see we've all come out to meet you!" the man roared.

"Jack, meet Bharat," Angus said. "He's the chief forest warden."

Jack looked up into Bharat's dark eyes.

Bharat winked. "I went to college with Angus," he said, "so I know what he's like. Hope he's treating you well. Here's my wife, Purnima, and little dribbling Shiv." He quickly handed the damp toddler over to Purnima, adding, "And Mila and Mina have been waiting all day to see you."

"Namaste!" The two girls bowed, hands together. They looked serious, but their eyes were dancing with friendliness.

They dragged Jack into the house, tugging and chattering. Jack had no choice about it. They didn't seem to notice his silence, and chattered on as they showed him around. Angus, Bharat and Purnima settled down in the lounge to catch up on old times and discuss Angus's plans.

Later, when Purnima had shooed the girls to their rooms, Jack escaped outside. He squatted on the steps, holding the wooden elephant, glad to have time to himself.

Suddenly, a monkey swung down from the veranda roof, snatched the elephant from Jack's hand, and ran off across the lawn. Jack raced after it.

Reaching a fence post, the monkey tried to take a bite out of its catch, then shrieked and jabbered in disgust. This thing was hard, not soft or juicy at all. The monkey flung the useless fruit away. Strings trailing, the small wooden elephant rolled across the lawn towards a large stone, set in the grass.

Jack ran over, then stopped and bent down. The stone's surface was inscribed with an elegant flowing script. As Jack ran his finger over the letters, a shadow darkened the stone. Bharat was standing behind him.

"You're wondering what that stone is there for?" Bharat said, echoing Jack's unspoken question. "Let me tell you. It is in memory of two great spirits."

Jack looked up, interested, and Bharat nodded, smiling gently.

"When my father was about your own age, still a boy, he chose to work with elephants, though our family was not poor. He worked for an old mahout, doing the hardest tasks. Each day, the mahout made him collect heaps of leaves and shoots, because elephants have huge appetites, and must be fed. He learnt how to wash elephants and scrub them clean. He learnt how to care for their skin, and about all the herbs that heal elephant sicknesses and injuries. Gradually, the old man shared all his skills because he knew my father could be trusted. By the time I was born, my father was a famous mahout himself, known for his wisdom and love of elephants."

Bharat picked up the small wooden elephant. "Look, five toes on his front feet, and four on the back. This little one was made with care. Whoever created him must have loved elephants too." He placed the carving in Jack's hands.

"But let me finish my tale. One day, my father found a beautiful, good-natured elephant, and he became her mahout. For thirty years there was a great love between them, and when she died, he never forgot her. So when, at last, my father died, I set up this stone to honour their two kindred spirits." Bharat pointed to the carved script and shook his head. "It says *For Ever*, Jack. Ah, if only! The world is a hard place for elephants now. All I can do is work, in his memory, to save them as best I can."

Hesitantly, Jack put his hand out and touched Bharat's arm. They stood there in silence, then walked back towards the house. Angus met them coming up the steps, and for a second, Jack thought he looked quite hurt, almost as if he was jealous.

The tiny mouse squeezed itself desperately through the shutters, panting. He glanced at the small elephant and staggered over, leaning breathlessly against his wooden side. Outside, a bird swept backwards and forwards, screeching eerily as it

hunted for prey. The mouse held a paw to its panting chest.

"Hope you don't mind, grand sir," he gasped. "I just need to rest for a moment. Do not take offence."

The elephant's carved smile seemed to grow larger. "Rest as long as you need to, little one. Wait till it is safe for you to run."

Jack clambered into the back of the jeep with Mina and Mila.

"Hurry, hurry, Daddy! We're late!" the girls cried.

Angus got in beside Bharat, and the jeep set off along the winding road. As the trees thinned out, Jack saw rows of women in bright saris, working in the plantations far below.

After a while, they arrived at a simple building with a thatched roof. It was the school. Outside, in the shade of a big banyan tree, a group of children sat reciting from a blackboard. The teacher caught sight of Bharat's jeep and stopped.

Mina and Mila ran to join their class, dragging Jack with them. Suddenly, to his horror, more than sixty faces turned towards him. Some of the kids pointed at the dangling wooden elephant and some giggled. Jack tried to back away.

"Please will you answer some of our questions?" asked the teacher, gently.

Heart thumping, Jack realized the teacher was talking to him. What could he do? If he spoke now, in public, it would be even harder not to talk to Angus. In fact, it was a trick, Jack was sure of it. That's why he'd been brought here. No, he could not, *would not* speak, not even when the teacher asked him.

Jack shook his head rudely, violently, panicking. Angus and Bharat were watching him, and Mila and Mina too. Everybody was watching. He could not bear it. Jack lifted his fists, as if to push the teacher away, and his eyes blazed angrily.

Bharat stepped in, putting a calming hand on Jack's shoulder. "Jack doesn't like talking," he told the children and the teacher.

"Ah! Shy," they whispered, understandingly.

One of the boys put up a hand and made a short speech.

"Thank you, Ravinder," said the teacher, translating. "He says that you have a beautiful elephant with you, Jack, so you should not feel afraid."

Another child put up his arm, and then another. "They hope you enjoy your time here. They hope that when you are back in England you will send us a postcard."

Jack looked at all the friendly faces, refusing to let the tears rise in his eyes.

"I know," the teacher beamed, "we'll sing Jack one of our favourite songs…"

Jack sniffed, wiped his nose and lifted his head.

Angus was frowning at him, as if he was disappointed. Jack glared back, and turned away.

A beeping horn attracted everyone's attention. A truck drew up and a warden rushed over to Bharat, speaking rapidly.

"There's trouble at one of the logging camps," Bharat explained. "Someone's been hurt. We must go. Sorry!" he said, bowing slightly to the puzzled school children.

Roughly, Angus bundled Jack back into the jeep.

As soon as the jeep whirled into the camp, Bharat leapt out and ran over to the tents with his medicine bag.

"You! Stay here! Right?" Angus said, coldly.

Jack waited alone, by the jeep. He could see the cluster of angry loggers, making wild gestures as they described what had happened. A huge bull elephant — a tusker, they said — had charged at the man and lifted him on its tusks, they said. It would have trampled him if they hadn't attacked it with sticks and guns. Jack turned the small elephant over and over in his hands, trying to block out the terrified voices as they told and retold the story.

Angus and Bharat came back. "What a lucky man. He'll have a bad headache from the fall, but at least he's only got a dislocated shoulder and bruising," Bharat said, as they set off in the jeep again. "It could have been a lot worse. These lone elephants often end up rampaging through the farmers' crops, destroying huts and homes and lives."

"Not their fault, though, is it?" muttered Angus, speaking only to Bharat. "When there's not enough room for them any more?" He had given up speaking to Jack.

Later that day, things got even worse for Jack. After supper, Purnima offered him a treat, a dish of freshly prepared jellabies.

He didn't mean to be rude, but by now he felt as if not speaking was like a stiff thick coat that kept him tightly inside its folds. Awkwardly, Jack shook his head at her and raised his fists to keep her away.

"Jack! Go to your room," shouted Angus, exasperated. "Go! Now!"

Jack swung out of his chair, stormed to his room and buried his head in the pillow. He could hear Angus apologizing to the family.

"I'm sorry, Purnima. He's like that all the time. I've tried and tried, but I don't know how much more I can take. I don't want this. I don't."

The small elephant heard the voices in the house grow quiet. After a while, Purnima crept into the bedroom. She placed a tin on the table, and a covered flask of water. She pulled the covers over Jack's bed and adjusted the mosquito net around him. The boy did not move, but his hands were still clenched in anger, and she was not sure if he was asleep.

"Goodnight, Jack," she whispered, as she left. He did not reply.

Time passed and the third elephant kept watch. The boy lay unmoving, like a carved figure in the bed, his body tight with rage.

A motherly rat padded her way across to the small elephant. Her fur was faded and her old eyes were calm and wise. The rat patted the small elephant's wooden trunk, nodded reassuringly, and moved on.

Then three little mice pattered in. They circled the floor, hoping for food. Suddenly they squeaked and scurried away.

"Did you hear him, elephant? Did you?"

The small elephant saw that Jack was looking at him with those intense eyes.

"Did you hear what that man said? Don't want this! Now I know for sure. He doesn't want me, and I don't want him. Don't want him at all, ever. Being alone is OK, isn't it? Being someone who doesn't feel, who doesn't care? You must know that, elephant."

For a while, the whole room seemed full of Jack's silent fury.

Then Jack sat up and threw back the covers. He switched on the light and got out of bed.

He opened Purnima's tin. Inside lay some of the troublesome jellabies, dusted with sugar. Jack didn't want any sweetness now. He closed the lid. Then he grasped the wooden elephant tightly.

"I've decided," Jack said, his eyes blazing. "If Angus doesn't want me, I don't want to stay. But you're coming with me."

Jack tugged on his clothes and found his torch. Then he crept through the sleeping house and stepped silently into the darkness of the night.

He walked across the lawn, past the elephant stone, and took the paved path into the forest. He did not care, even when the path narrowed and turned to earth. The moon was full, casting a silver light, showing him where he was going. Jack was so angry that the rustlings in the trees did not bother him, nor the snufflings of hidden creatures, nor the huge moths fluttering about.

Don't want this, don't want this, he thought, striding along. That's what Angus had said. What Angus meant was that he didn't want *him*. He couldn't stand Jack any more.

After a while, Jack's pace slowed. The path divided, meandering off into darker spaces under the trees so he couldn't see where to go. He pushed forward and forward and eventually came out onto a new track. But which way should he turn?

The moon clouded over until all Jack could see was a quivering circle of fading torchlight in the dark, dark forest. He remembered tales of tigers leaping down from overhanging branches, tearing a man's scalp from his head with a swipe of a paw.

His rage left him and he began to feel very alone. He looked around, backing up against a tree. Trying to forget about snakes and poisonous spiders, he crouched down. This was not a place he wanted to be, not any more.

The small elephant could feel the boy shaking. "Listen," Jack whispered. "I've done something stupid. I'll go back when it's lighter. Maybe nobody will have noticed."

Slowly, slowly, the night sky lightened and black shadows changed to morning mists. Distant birds screeched at the early dawn. Jack scratched wherever insects bit, and tried not to panic.

The small elephant could do nothing. "Keep him safe," he thought. "Keep Jack safe."

And then it happened. At first it was a scent, a smell, something on the breeze that alerted them. Then, almost silently, along the track appeared a small herd of elephants, one behind another.

As the herd grew level, Jack felt as if he could stretch out a hand and touch their wrinkled skin. The huge mothers moved almost like great grey clouds, tall and mighty, blocking out the pale dawn sky above the crouching boy.

Young ones and babies trotted alongside, some linking trunk or tail with their mothers, all passing along the ancient elephant track to a new feeding ground. They made hardly any sound. All Jack could hear was their gentle breathing, and soft snorts and rumbles, sent like messages up and down the herd. Only one baby elephant paused, astonished, eyeing the hidden watcher curiously, until a low call made him trot after the herd once more.

Jack watched the herd move through the forest, searching for food and freedom. He watched until they had gone, then settled down again. Morning was coming fast and soon he would find his way back.

The small elephant was amazed by what he had seen. How wonderful! How magnificent!

He thought of his own round self in the mouse's mirror, days before. Had he, who fitted in the palm of a hand, truly been made to look like one of these grey giants who roamed free? It was unbelievable. Once he had stood in a dusty room, wishing to see a pretty white palace, when all the time there was something far greater to see. People had often called him a lucky elephant, but at this moment he felt far more than that.

* * *

All at once, Jack heard someone shouting.

It was Angus. "Jack, where are you? Jack? Jack?" he called.

They heard him thundering through the trees and blundering through the bushes. Then Angus burst out of the forest, further along the track. He looked this way and that, searching the pale morning shadows. "Where are you, Jack?" Angus shouted, then groaned and folded his head in his hands. "Please?"

Jack froze. Angus's shouts reminded him how badly he'd behaved to the children at the school, and to Purnima. He stayed still as stone.

Then he saw something moving further up the track – a vast bull elephant, tusks swaying with each step. It had picked up the scent of the herd and was following their trail, ready to trample anything in its path. Angus, crouching, had not seen it.

Horrified, Jack clutched the carved elephant tighter. He must do something, but he had been silent so long. He gave a quick thin croak, as if his voice was locked away, and all the time the elephant was coming closer to Angus.

"Do it, Jack, do it!" The boy seemed to hear a small wooden voice sounding in his mind. "Tell him now!"

Jack gasped, gulped down air, and though he felt his throat cracking, yelled out with all his might. "Angus!" he shouted "Angus, Angus! Watch out!"

Angus heard the shout and lifted his head, astonished. He saw Jack gesturing frantically and then he

saw the huge elephant advancing along the track.

Leaping to his feet, Angus raced as fast he could towards Jack. He grabbed him and flung them both off the path, away among the trees. They rolled down into a hollow and lay there, not daring to move.

The great elephant thundered to a stop close by them, its massive ears stretched out wide, and its trunk raised threateningly. Its eyes gleamed, aware of the danger that might be around and the dangers it had already known. Its leathery hide was covered with scars and swollen sores.

The huge beast's mighty feet trampled the ground. It swayed from side to side, as if getting ready to charge. Then it seized a fallen branch, thrashed it about above its head, and smashed it to splinters on the ground. With a triumphant bellow, it headed off along the track.

Jack and Angus relaxed, and stared at each other. The small elephant heard them breathe the same sigh of relief, as if they did not trust themselves to speak.

After a moment, Jack moved. "Ouch!" Something hard and round was sticking into his ribs. He reached down and picked up the wooden elephant. As he held up the carved creature, he saw something he had never noticed before, in all the time he had carried it around: the small elephant's cheerful, curved smile, full of friendliness and hope. Jack grinned.

"What?" Angus said, puzzled.

Jack held the carving out to show him. He tipped the

wooden elephant backwards and forwards. The smile grew bigger and smaller, as if the carving was laughing, and soon they were both laughing too.

"Come on." Angus smiled, struggling up and brushing the leaves and small twigs off his clothes. "Time to get back to the house."

"OK," Jack answered, and they went back along the path together.

The small elephant was on the sill, looking out through the shutters at the birds swooping from branch to branch in the forest. He could hear the hum of voices as Jack and Angus and the others sat chatting in the other room.

With a squeeze and a scrabble, two rather elderly mice pushed in through the slats. They studied the small elephant with interest.

"So," they asked, "did you see him? Did you see the great beast? And is he not the wonder of the world? Better than moonlight on palaces? Better than marble or glittering stones?"

"That and more, dear mice," he said. "But he is so great and I am nothing but a carved thing."

"Oh, little wooden elephant," they giggled. *"Don't you come from the forest, like the mighty elephant? Doesn't anyone with a heart look at you and remember the living elephants? Be quiet. Be at peace. All is well."*

All that morning, over and over, Mila and Mina made Jack tell his story of the angry elephant. To his relief, Angus didn't let on why they were both in the forest at dawn. When, at last, Purnima took them off to the kitchen, the girls gazed admiringly over their shoulders at Jack.

Angus leant across the table, and ruffled Jack's hair. "Listen, I've been so busy that I forgot to arrange this before now. I've chatted about it with Bharat and we've got it sorted. Can you be ready in an hour?"

"Yes," said Jack, a little puzzled.

Two figures were waiting at the end of the lawn. One was a young lad and the other a wizened, bow-legged man with a wide, toothless grin and an ankush. Between them stood a comfortable elephant with pretty mottled ears. She was tugging away with enjoyment at the frangipani blossoms.

"This is the boy?" the old man said.

"Yes, Gajendra, this is Jack," Bharat replied.

"Good. This is Missy, Jack. Baitho!" the mahout commanded. With a rumbling sigh, Missy knelt.

"Get on, then," Angus urged.

"Just me? Aren't you coming?"

"Not now, Jack. But I promise I will another time. Gajendra will take good care of you. And I want to hear all about Missy when you get back," Angus answered, laughing kindly.

Jack scrambled up on to the simple howdah and sat,

cross-legged. Gajendra followed, settling himself behind the elephant's head.

"Missy, *mylay!*" Gajendra shouted. The elephant stood up, then plodded off determinedly along one of the forest paths.

"OK?" the mahout said, grinning. Jack saw the man's feet were wedged behind the elephant's ears so that he could knead her neck and drive her along. "Missy is always obedient," Gajendra added, "though rather greedy, like all haathi."

After a while, Jack got used to the elephant's swaying, and relaxed his grip on the howdah's rim. The ground seemed far away and he could look down on the head of the mahout's boy.

The forest was a different place in the daytime. Birds, flashes of gold and blue and turquoise, swooped among the branches, giving long piercing calls. Spotted deer appeared and disappeared among the distant shadows. Monkeys jabbered and shrieked and leapt on the topmost branches. Butterflies swam around in the heavy air. The elephant plodded on, her ears flapping gently in rhythm with her steps. Occasionally she snatched tender young leaves, until Gajendra called out, making her move on.

Suddenly, with a snort, the elephant swung her trunk upwards and rummaged around where Jack was sitting, searching for hidden food. She discovered the small elephant, round as an apple, and lowered it towards her mouth.

"Don't!" Jack cried, recalling Princess cracking her coconut shells. "Please. It's not mine."

Gajendra gave a stream of commands. Slowly Missy uncoiled her trunk, wanting to see what she had been forbidden. She held the small elephant aloft, turning the miniature animal one way and another as if she were studying the small carving. Then, from deep within, came a rumbling, grumbling, snorting noise, something like an amused laugh.

The small elephant heard that mischievously happy sound and smiled too.

Gently, very gently, Missy lifted her trunk again and placed the small elephant back in Jack's out-stretched palm. Then she carried on her way, into a grove full of scarlet flowers.

"*Dhuth!* Missy, stop!" Gajendra cried as they drew near the house and plodded across the lawn. Everyone had gathered to see Jack arrive back. His eyes shone, and a long scarf was wrapped, turban-like, around his blond hair. Angus raised his camera and took a photo.

As Jack slid off the elephant's back, the mahout's boy gave him a bamboo leaf parcel, oozing with stickiness and with a rich, treacle-sweet smell. At once, Missy's eyes twinkled. She moved adoringly towards Jack.

"Quick, Jack, you'd better reward her for your ride," Bharat said.

"What is it?" Jack asked.

"Raw molasses. Gur. It's Missy's special treat…"

And the gur was gone, swiftly popped inside a widely opened pink mouth. As Missy chewed, her small eyes closed in contented delight.

A row of mice appeared on the sill. They stared at the small elephant with large luminous eyes and nudged each other anxiously.

"Good evening," they said. "We have something to ask you. Have we done well enough?"

"Pardon?"

"Have we mice accompanied you well on your wish?"

"Oh yes, you have done well," the small elephant said. "Please give my thanks to all in the mouse world for their help. It would have been a lonely journey without your assistance."

The tiniest mouse stepped forward. "One more thing, please. Do tell. You were not frightened by us mice, small elephant, like they say in the stories?"

"No." The wooden elephant laughed. "Maybe the snake frightened me in my dark time. But frightened of you, dear mice? Impossible."

The city air was dusty, sour, full of gathering excitement. The cab sped Jack and Angus through the raucous traffic, across the wide river and squealed into a parking place.

"Is this your final sight?" asked the cab driver.

"Yes. This, and then home," Angus told him, handing over rupees.

"Pity. It's almost the big festival," the driver said. "But home is home."

Angus and Jack stood on the pavement, waiting and yawning. It was very late. Above them, planes destined for other lands glinted in the night sky. Here it was quieter, almost as if the air itself was waiting.

Dr Singh, another of Angus's friends, slid through the gathering crowd to greet them. "I've got the permits. Are you ready?" he asked.

"Yes, thanks," Angus said. "Keep close, Jack, won't you?"

"Sure. Of course," the boy replied.

"This way, this way!" Dr Singh called, hurrying them from the harsh glow of streetlights to a darker place. Faint floodlights showed them the way and uni-formed guides made sure all visitors were heading in the right direction.

The small elephant heard feet shuffling on the stones around them as they passed through a huge arched gateway into another courtyard, then through another arch. Then there they were. And there it was.

The small elephant saw a star twinkling in the sky, and a moon, and then, where the ribbon of silver water ended, he saw his lovely white palace. Only it was not his miniature palace, but a vast and wonderful building that glowed softly, more beautiful than he could ever have imagined.

Gradually, the soft floodlights dimmed and all was darkness. Everyone waited for dawn to arrive. As the sun broke over the city, calls to prayer pierced the drone of endless traffic.

"Look, little one," whispered Jack. "The Taj Mahal."

Then the wooden elephant saw the wonderful palace reappear, misty grey, then rose pink, then gold, until it blazed out in perfect whiteness again. The jewelled patterns shone around the dome and the minarets stood like tall pillars of light. As he watched, the path of water turned from silver to liquid gold to the blue of the daylight sky above. Not a small white palace, but an enormous white palace. A wonder of the world!

* * *

Angus watched the Taj Mahal reveal its beauty, then turned to look at Jack. He thought of all the things they had talked about on their long journey towards this place: about that strange little elephant, and how Jack had become his friend, something he had feared would never happen.

Now the boy stood there, eyes wide open with amazement, holding up that small elephant as if it could see too. As Jack looked across at him, and grinned, Angus clicked his camera.

THE FOURTH ELEPHANT

DIWALI! IT WAS THE FESTIVAL THAT NANJI LOVED, and she showed it by bossing everyone unmercifully, even Mum.

"We must get ready properly," she insisted.

She made them clean the place from top to bottom, including, to Nita's horror, their bedrooms. She made Mum check that all the lights were ready, from the boxes of clay diwali lamps to the new electric lights for the front porch. She watched every stroke that Sara made, chalking the rangoli pattern across the front doorstep so that everyone who arrived during the festival would be welcomed. She made Mum take them all shopping so they had new clothes to wear to celebrate the festival and welcome the new year. The kitchen and the fridge were filled with endless food, and whenever they had a break, Nanji would tell them tales of her long-ago childhood.

In between, she would chat on the phone, making sure that all her friends, whoever they were, would be visiting. "It's Diwali, isn't it? You must come," she told some. "It's like your Christmas, only better!" she explained to others.

At last Diwali arrived. Nanji had brought out all her own favourite decorations and put lights all round the painting of the beautiful blue flute-player. The tiny flat was crowded with people and laughter. Sara had never seen so many pairs of shoes left in their downstairs hall before.

Nanji kept telling everyone about Nita's bike ride.

"What a heroine she was, and she returned safely, so this year the lights are for her, as well as for the triumphant return of Rama and Sita."

Sara wasn't left out of the praise. Nanji told everyone that her youngest granddaughter had been chosen to play at the Celebration Concert in London.

Nanji enjoyed herself tremendously, especially when she won at cards. She put some of her winnings under the flower vase in her golden corner. "Here's some cash to say thank you to our lovely Goddess Lakshmi for all the luck we had last year, and for all the luck we hope she'll give us for the next!" she cried.

Sara loved Diwali, but all of a sudden she was fed up with hearing about luck and the Celebration Concert. Going to her room, she got her flute out of its case. The silvery instrument gleamed in her hands, but she was getting more and more nervous. She could not forget that Nita had lost her lucky elephant, even though she'd been really sorry.

"Sara," said Nita, peeping around the door. "I've got something to show you." Sara looked suspicious. "You'll be glad," promised Nita.

She sat Sara down in front of the computer, pressed a key, and there on the screen was a photo of the Taj Mahal.

"So?" sulked Sara. "So what? I've already seen your photos."

"This isn't mine," said Nita, clicking eagerly to the next image. There was a boy, grinning, and in his hands was a small wooden elephant. Could it be...?

Sara clicked again. An unfamiliar voice crackled through the speakers. "Hello. Jack here. This is a picture of your elephant at the Taj Mahal. Don't we look great? Be in touch soon. Jack." The audioclip ended.

"That's him? My elephant?" Sara gasped. "The lucky, lucky thing!"

"I wanted it to be a surprise for you," Nita said.

Then Nita explained, which took some time, how the boy had sent messages through the bike ride website, and she'd emailed back, and then his sort-of-stepfather Angus had helped Jack put the photograph and the message together so that Sara could see her lost elephant again.

"It's a fantastic surprise, Nita. But will my elephant be home in time for the concert?"

Nita laughed. "You don't need it, silly. You can play brilliantly by yourself, you know. But, yes, the small elephant will be certainly be home by then."

The huge hall was filling up. Mr Green pushed along the row, into his seat, and looked up, past the ornate gold carvings and the forest of organ pipes. He ignored the stupid discs intended to improve the sound and saw only the vast blue dome above. He suddenly felt as if he had more than a touch of the butterflies under his own best waistcoat buttons.

He remembered the terror on Sara's face as she arrived for rehearsal that morning and saw the round domed building with its Victorian carvings. But Miss Mackenzie had soon calmed her down.

Now it was the moment, the real thing. Sara was waiting somewhere in the wings with the rest of the orchestra. Soon she would be coming up onto the stage. No doubt that Lauren girl was making a fuss about not playing the solo, but he knew his Saraswati was the better musician, by a long way.

Now her family was arriving. He shifted in his seat and beamed politely. There was her mother and the grandmother, Nanji, and that spiky-haired sister who had gone on an expedition somewhere. Then three more people joined them, causing another bustle of welcomes.

"Angus and Jack, and Jack's mother, Rosie," he heard Sara's mum saying as she introduced the small family.

For heaven's sake! Mr Green's fixed smile became somewhat sterner. Did they not know that the concert he'd worked so hard for was about to start? The concert where his star pupil would be playing her flute? A round of applause broke out as the musicians walked onto the stage and took their places.

Mr Green tutted with annoyance. He could not believe it. What was that Jack boy doing now? Why exactly had he brought that wretched wooden elephant along, and why was he holding it up towards Sara, distracting her? Sara looked anxious enough already. He growled and tapped his programme briskly.

Sara sat high up on the platform. She gulped, and lifted her head and saw all her family sitting in a row. Then she saw Jack, leaping up and down, and grinning madly. He was holding her wooden elephant, waving it about and pointing at it like a daft, friendly fool.

All at once, Sara's face lit up with happiness and she felt fine again. Even when the lights dimmed, the hall hushed and the concert began.

And when the time for the solo came, and the conductor lifted his baton, Sara played as if she was in a wonderful dream.

It was late when they got out of the station.

"A cab tonight, I think," said Mum. "It's too far to walk home."

"And much too late. This young one is nearly asleep," said Nanji, her arm around Sara.

Into the taxi they piled – Mum, Nanji, Nita and Sara, with her flute and her wooden elephant. She smiled sleepily. It had been a fantastic day.

She'd really enjoyed meeting Jack and his family. They'd promised to see each other again soon, because she wanted to hear about all his adventures and all about the elephants. It had been a magical evening.

Nanji made Sara put the small elephant on the back windowshelf, along with her flute, so they could all be comfortable in the taxi.

"It's such a long ride home," said Nanji. "Please, do you know any short cuts?"

The driver's short cut led the cab to a set of emergency lights and roadworks instead.

"Sorry about the wait," the cab driver said, turning on his radio.

Nanji raised her eyes and tapped him smartly on the shoulder. "Sssh!" she hissed. "We have had a long, long day, thank you. Peace and quiet is what we need."

The small elephant gazed out of the back window. On that particular stretch of pavement, just where the cab was waiting, was a dingy shop. Its windows were crammed with second-hand objects and discarded sheet music and several stacks of rather dusty books. As a passing bus lit up the windows, the small elephant stared. And then he stared again.

Among the muddle on display, there were two rather battered wooden elephants, used as a pair of bookends. One was certainly large and the other was certainly less so. Their small eyes gazed blankly through the glass, as if this was all they had ever bothered wishing for, and they were contented enough.

The small elephant smiled, and the cab moved on.

Nanji wanted to sleep, but she was restless. Today had been one of the best days of her life. She sighed, wishing her son had been there to see his daughter playing her flute.

She thought about Angus, and Rosie, and that nice boy, Jack. He was so young, yet he had been all the way to India, just like her clever Nita. There was some funny mystery about Sara's wooden elephant, which had also gone all the way to India and back again, but Nanji wasn't sure what it was all about.

Sara had been so happy to have the small wooden elephant back home. She had put him back in Nanji's golden corner, where he had often stood before his adventures. There he was, right by that big vase of flowers. And look at the flowers, fading already!

Suddenly, Nanji rose to her feet. It was time to sort out that vase.

As Nanji moved the vase away, the small wooden elephant looked across the shining golden cloth and could not believe what he saw. There, facing him, was the family gift that Nita had brought back from her travels. The small elephant was looking at a most marvellous figure, a magical person.

This person was seated on a throne. He had a comfortably rounded human tummy and a human body and — could it be true? — the wise, wise head of an elephant!

The smile on his elephant face was the kindest and cheeriest in the whole wide world, and the tusk held in his hand

seemed almost like a pen writing a wonderful tale. By one foot, just as if it was listening to every word of a marvellous story, was a tiny carved mouse-like creature.

Suddenly, the small elephant felt surrounded by the warmth of a great and generous spirit. He felt as if he was trembling, as if some miracle had happened, and in his ears he heard the sounds of many mighty elephants calling in the far-off forests of India, calling out their triumphant cries as the world changed about them. His head was filled with dreams, not of palaces, but of leaves and trees and forests...

"Ah, small elephant." Nanji smiled, as she placed a flickering diva-lamp in front of the holy image. "Now you have met the great God Ganesha, to whom nothing is impossible, whether hopes or wishes or dreams."

ACKNOWLEDGEMENTS

All the characters in *The Third Elephant* are imaginary, and are not intended to represent any person, living or dead, or any person who shares the same or a similar name. The places and setting are my own fictional interpretations of the varied landscapes and sights of India, and so I apologize if there are any errors of fact or geography or customs or culture within my story.

Many thanks to Sonia and Daniel Benster, Saraswati Basker, Alan and Millie Cummings, John and Margaret Pegg, and Paul Williams, whose generously shared knowledge about India, elephants and all manner of interesting things makes this story a richer experience for the reader than it would have been without their help. I must also thank the Chave-Cox family, the Knight family and the Sanghvi family for informal insights into the world of lessons, practices, rehearsals and concerts that shapes the lives of young musicians.

Among the authors of the many books I read for this story, I must particularly acknowledge and thank the travel writer Mark Shand, whose wonderful accounts of his Indian journeys *Travels on My Elephant* and *Queen of the Elephants* (Penguin Books) were both an inspiration and an education.

As a writer, I was lucky to have comments on an early version of my story from young readers at Beckwithshaw Primary School, North Yorkshire, who were especially keen on elephant riding. I was also glad to receive wise suggestions, support and encouragement from Bernie Crosthwaite, Jamila Gavin, Ruth Elwin Harris, Hilary Robinson, Sarah Storey and Jo Williams at various points in my struggles with the "elephant idea", and I send my warmest thanks to all of you.

I would also like to thank the many people who helped to turn my manuscript into a book, beginning with my agent, Pat White, of Rogers, Coleridge & White, for her care and interest, and especially her enthusiasm for my rather different style of story. My gratitude to all the team at Walker Books for their skill and help, with very special thanks to my editor Caroline Royds for all her subtle patience and kindness in guiding my words and story. I must also include my grateful thanks to the artist and illustrator Helen Craig, whose wonderful pictures have added so much magic to *The Third Elephant*.

Last, but never ever least, my most enormous thanks go to my family, especially the great Jim Dolan, whose unique brand of help and support goes way, way beyond looking after my computer.

Penny Dolan, Summer 2006

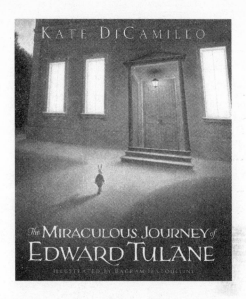

Once, in a house on Egypt Street, there lived a
china rabbit named Edward Tulane. The rabbit was
very pleased with himself, and for good reason: he
was owned by a girl named Abilene, who treated him
with the utmost care and adored him completely.
And then, one day, he was lost.

Kate DiCamillo takes us on an extraordinary
journey, from the depths of the ocean to the net
of a fisherman, from the top of a garbage heap to the
fireside of a hoboes' camp, from the bedside of an
ailing child to the streets of Memphis. And along
the way, we are shown a true miracle – that
even a heart of the most breakable kind can
learn to love, to lose, and to love again.